# THE DARK AND ITS CHARMS

*a serial killer thriller*

## PHINEAS AND LIAM, BOOK ONE

V. J. Chambers

Punk Rawk Books

# THE DARK AND ITS CHARMS

*a serial killer thriller*

## PHINEAS AND LIAM, BOOK ONE

V. J. Chambers

# CHAPTER ONE

Haysle Dawson knocked on the door of the apartment and then wished she hadn't.

*I'm not ready to talk to him,* she thought frantically.

She turned to look over her shoulder, down the hallway of the apartment building. Rows of identical doors stretched out towards the door to the parking lot, where she was parked. The files on this case were sitting on her passenger seat, and she wished she had one more chance to look through them, one more chance to try to formulate what it was exactly she wanted to say.

Maybe she could run, disappear back to the car and come back in twenty minutes after she'd boned up on the file on last time.

*He won't think I was the person who knocked on his door and ran, will he?*

The door to the apartment opened.

Too late. There he was.

She recognized him, but he looked better than he did in the photos in the file, probably because the photos had been taken after he'd been locked underground in a dog crate by a serial killer for weeks on end. She expected that didn't really contribute to people looking their best.

He looked younger and cleaner. Better groomed, even though he still had a little bit of stubble on his chin and jaw. He was even attractive, she decided, not that she should be finding him attractive. That was incredibly inappropriate.

"Can I help you?" he said.

"Mr. Liam Emerson?" she said.

He registered the typical surprise everyone did when hearing her voice, which was low, very low, too low for a woman. "Yes, that's me."

She fumbled around in her back pocket, trying to get out her badge. "I'm with, um, the Cape Christopher Police Department." There. She held up her badge triumphantly. "I'm Detective Haysle Dawson."

To his credit, he seemed to have gotten past her deep voice quickly enough. "Did something happen? With Finn?"

"Sort of," she said.

"Did he hurt someone?" His voice was tight.

"No, no, nothing like that," she said. "Don't worry. It's nothing… dangerous. Well… I don't know. Maybe, depending on your point of view, it could be…" What was she saying? "But no, it's not. At all."

He raised his eyebrows.

She let out a little laugh. "Would it be possible for me to come inside?"

He hesitated.

"I should have called first," she said. "I was going to, but sometimes, on the phone…" People misgendered her on the phone, all the time, and it wasn't the way she wanted to make her first impression. She was confusing enough in that regard without making it worse. At least when people saw her, they saw a female, and that made it easier.

Well, not that she really cared.

She did care somewhat, she supposed. If she hadn't cared, then she would still be taking testosterone supplements and answering to the first name Hayes. So, she cared. It mattered. But whether people looked at her and saw a male or a female person, it didn't change the essence of who she was. In that sense, she was above it all.

"I'm sorry," she said. "I should have called."

He squared his shoulders. "It's only that, um, thinking about Finn, it can be… upsetting."

"Oh, of course," she said. "How could it not be? He captured you. He kept you prisoner. He treated you like an animal. What you went through, it must have been—" She cringed. "Something you probably wish I wouldn't have enumerated like that." Damn it. Why hadn't she run back to the car? Why hadn't she prepared for this better?

The truth was that she didn't understand why she'd been put on this case. It was her first assignment at the Cape Christopher Police Department, and she thought it was a bit odd. Usually, people didn't think of her as the type to sweet-talk civilians into helping the cops. But she wasn't going to question her first assignment. She was going to do her best and she was going to secure Liam Emerson's help. She had to succeed at this. She couldn't fail right out of the gate. But if she'd rubbed him the wrong way, she wouldn't push either.

She licked her lips. "Maybe now's not a good time. You want to tell me when I should come back? Or if you'd rather I didn't come to your house, we could meet somewhere, maybe a coffee shop or something in town?"

He smirked. "And keep me in suspense about what this is all about? I think I'll get an ulcer that way. Nah, you can come on in. Just… don't mind the mess." He stepped away from the door.

She crossed the threshold.

The apartment opened onto a living room, but this living room didn't have a couch or anything like that. Instead, it had a desk with several monitors sitting on it, and a bean bag chair slouching in the corner. There were bags from fast food restaurants, grease stains on the bottom, littering the floor.

She tried not to wince, thinking about getting grease

out of the carpet. The carpet was a mix of browns and blacks, however, the kind of thing that hid dirt fairly well. She smiled. "What mess?"

He chuckled. "Uh, we can sit in the kitchen. There's a table in there."

"Whatever you think is best," she said.

He took off through a doorway, and she followed him.

There was indeed a table in the kitchen—which was spotless, as if no one used it for anything, either cooking or eating—a small table with two straight back chairs.

Liam pulled out one and gestured for her to sit as well. "I guess you know that I, um, make YouTube videos for a living."

"Oh, right, I remember that now," said Dawson. "About that vampire movie?"

"TV show," he said. "*How To Get Away with Magic.*"

"I don't think I've ever seen that," she said.

"It's canceled now," he said. "It hasn't been on the air since 2013."

"Oh," she said, raising her eyebrows. "But people watch videos about that still?"

He laughed. "They do." He set his hands palms down on the table. "Not to rush you, but can we get into what this is about?"

"Oh, of course," she said, taking a deep breath. "Well, I don't know if you're aware, but Phineas Slater has confessed to more murders."

Liam rubbed his forehead. "I wish I could say I was surprised, but the truth is, I'm not. "

"It's not uncommon for serial killers to do this," said Dawson. "But with little deterrent to confessing and the reward of deeper notoriety and more attention, they often confess to murders they didn't actually commit. So, there could be more bodies, or maybe it's an elaborate game that Slater is playing. We really can't be sure."

"You think he's lying about there being more

murders?" said Liam. "Because, I have to tell you, I don't. Didn't he indicate that there were two other murders in college? He told me that he tried to pin them on me."

"We're well aware he was trying to frame you. Don't worry. You're not a suspect."

"I know I'm not," said Liam. "That's not what I'm saying."

"He didn't confess to old murders," said Dawson. "Anyway, where did you go to college?"

"Delaware."

"That's not our jurisdiction," she said. "These murders he's confessed to, he's saying they're in this area, and that they're recent."

"I don't understand," he said. "Jurisdiction? There were FBI agents involved in this case before. I thought the FBI handled serial killers."

"That's a common misconception," said Dawson. "The FBI provides assistance, but each police department conducts its own investigation."

"But they were here, and they were providing assistance."

"You're talking about Wren Delacroix and Caius Reilly?"

"Yes. Are they going to investigate in Delaware?"

"I think they go wherever the FBI directs them to go."

"Bullshit," he muttered. "The whole thing is bullshit. Listen, if Finn says he killed people, he killed people. Take him seriously. Don't assume he's lying."

"I'm not..." She lifted both of her hands, an I-surrender gesture. "I think I've explained this wrong. We don't think he's lying. We just don't know. We need evidence one way or another to charge him with further murders."

Liam lifted his chin. "You need bodies."

"Yes," she said.

"He won't tell you where the bodies are?"

"He doesn't want to tell us," she said. "He asked for you."

Liam's lips parted and all the blood drained out of his face.

She took a deep breath. "It's not conventional, but they asked me to approach you and see if you would be willing to help out. We can just as easily tell him that he can't talk to you, and that there's no deal." *Way to go. That's really convincing him to help here, giving him an out.* She was terrible at this. They should have given this job to anyone besides her.

"Okay," he said. "Then tell him that." He got up from the table.

"Well, if there are bodies?" she said, getting to her feet as well. "The families of the victims will want closure."

Liam hung his head. His voice was strained. "Tell him no. Tell him I don't want to see him. Tell him I'm *never* going to be near him again. And he'll eventually get bored and want attention, like you said. He'll crack and give the information to someone else. You don't need me."

"I realize it's a lot to ask," she murmured. "I'm sure what you went through was traumatizing and—"

"I can't." He raised his gaze to hers. "Sorry."

Her shoulders slumped. "Maybe you want to think about it. Maybe I can call you in a few days and you can give me an answer then."

"The answer is no." His voice was shaking.

"Maybe you'll feel differently in a few days," she said again.

He shook his head.

She reached into the pocket inside her suit jacket. "I'll give you my card. Call me if you have any questions or if you want to talk or if you change your mind." She pulled out a card and offered it to him.

He didn't take it.

She set it on the table. This had gone worse than she'd imagined.

"Is there anything else?" he said.

"No, that's all."

"Then I'll walk you out."

She sighed. "Thanks. I think I remember the way."

She saw herself out of the apartment then trudged down the row of identical doors toward the door to the parking lot.

Getting into her car, she swore under her breath.

Liam was right, anyway. Getting him involved in this? One of Slater's victims? It would be far too hard on the man.

The truth was that everyone at the CCPD treated Slater differently than they should, owing to the fact that he'd been a detective on the force, in both narcotics and later homicide, before he'd been caught.

Even though there was video of evidence of his raping the corpses of his victims, since he'd filmed himself doing it, there was a prevailing attitude toward him that seemed skeptical of his guilt. And he was treated better than he ought to be treated, at least that was what Dawson thought.

He had been a police officer, so he was kept away from other prisoners, who—it was thought—might retaliate against him. His whims were catered to with too much deference. And this request of his, to see Liam Emerson, was being carried out, at least attempted, anyway.

But it had failed.

*She* had failed.

And she could spend whatever time she wanted telling Captain Moore that she didn't think it was ethical to pressure Slater's victim to assist on an investigation, but he wouldn't care. He'd simply know that the first thing he'd asked her to accomplish, she hadn't accomplished.

So, that would be the second awkward conversation she'd had with the captain of the department, which meant things were off to an amazing start. The first awkward conversation had been about her gender, which was always the worst. She liked to avoid it when she could, because a lot of times she felt it revealed something ugly about people she was meeting and that cast a pall over their entire relationship from then on.

Maybe it was better to know it up front, she supposed.

The captain hadn't been too awful about it, admittedly, but she hadn't given him a chance, either.

She'd said, "Yes, I have a deep voice and an Adam's apple. No, I'm not a trans woman. I detransitioned. I identified as a woman until adolescence and then I thought that I identified as a man, but I was wrong. So, I went back to my birth gender."

The captain hadn't said anything. His mouth had been wide open.

She'd smiled. "Before you say anything, yes, there are people who *really are* trans. I just wasn't one of them." This was the thing that she found that people often wanted to say. They wanted to insinuate she'd been coerced into transitioning, as if someone out there had forced her to do it. They wanted her to speculate on how other trans people could be "fixed." It made her feel helpless rage. She wanted to scream that transitioning *did* fix trans people. It hadn't fixed her, but that was because she *wasn't* trans. "And no," she continued, "there's nothing I can do to make my voice change back. Once your voice drops, it drops."

The captain cleared his throat. "Well," he said. "Well, I think that's a very courageous story."

"Thank you," she said. She could see that there were one hundred questions on the tip of his tongue, things he wanted to know, and she hoped he wouldn't start asking them, because it was none of his business to know whether or not she'd had any surgeries. She hadn't. It was none of his business to know why she'd thought she was a man in the first place, and why she'd continued to live as a man for years after she'd realized that she actually probably wasn't one. It was none of his business why she'd decided to detransition at thirty years old, after over ten years on male hormones (well off and on, truly. She'd taken a few breaks here and there.) None of that was his business, and none of it was particularly easy to talk about.

She was lucky. The captain had only shaken her hand and that had been that. He hadn't said a word.

And then the information had been all around the entire department within a day, so she didn't have to "come out" to anyone else, which wasn't really the proper term for it, but she didn't know how else to put it.

So, now, that awkward part of getting a new job was done, and she could move forward.

Of course, it would be much easier to do if she hadn't flubbed her first assignment.

She leaned her head back against the head rest in her car and swore a few more times. Then, shaking her head, she put the keys in the ignition of her car and started it up. She pulled out of the parking lot and drove away.

# CHAPTER TWO

Liam's hands were shaking, and he kept dropping the bottle of Tylenol with codeine that he was trying to open.

He probably shouldn't have the codeine at all, but he'd whined a lot the last time he'd been at the doctor's office, and he'd somehow managed to finagle the doctor into handing him a bunch of samples, cautioning him that his prescriptions had run out, and that he needed to wean himself off these, which… well, Liam had full intentions of doing.

The bottle fell on the floor and the top came off. Pills spilled out over the linoleum in the kitchen, and he dropped down, desperately gathering them up and brushing at them to make sure they weren't covered in dirt or lint. Not that it would matter if they were. He would take them anyway.

He scooped them back into the bottle.

He probably shouldn't have been given any pain killers at all after he'd gotten free from Finn. After all, Finn hadn't hurt him physically. He wasn't the kind of serial killer who liked to carve people up and leave scars all over their bodies. He had tased Liam a lot, of course, especially that last day, and Liam had claimed to be having a lot of issues with the pain, and the Tylenol with codeine got handed out easily in the hospital and he left with a nice little prescription, with refills.

Liam was not stupid, so he began to notice that he was forming habits with the pills pretty quickly, and he knew that he should be careful.

He tried to summon the will to care about such things, but he found he couldn't.

Before Finn had caught him, maybe he might have. Things mattered back then, but nothing mattered now.

The pills knocked him out. He took them before he went to sleep at night, and then he slept in a pleasant little bubble of goodness. It was always the worst at night in the dark.

He wasn't sure why.

It had never been dark in the bunker, something he'd come to find out was because Finn was filming him at all times and wanted it light to have a good view of everything.

So, darkness didn't remind him of being held captive in that small, musty underground space. It didn't remind him of the dog crate where he'd been imprisoned for six weeks.

Even still, the dark was bad.

And sleeping with the lights on did remind him of the bunker. He wouldn't do that. It was too garish, and it made him feel as if he'd never left.

He couldn't bear the light and he feared the dark.

The pills helped.

He didn't take them except to sleep.

Well, not usually, anyway. Not often. Only once or twice a week did he take a pill during the day. Definitely not every day. Definitely not more than once a day.

He put one of the pills on his tongue, ran the sink, cupped his hand, and brought water to his mouth to swallow it. Water dribbled down his chin, through the beard he was not growing.

*I'm going to shave,* he told himself. *I'm allowed to shave now, since I'm not trapped in a bunker, and so I'm going to do it.*

But he didn't shave, at least not often.

He was busy making videos for his channel, except they weren't about *Hitgam*, (which was the phonetic way that fans rendered *HGTAM*, the initials of the show's title) and he hadn't released any of them yet.

They were all about *Dusk* and a fanfic of the work, called *This Love*, and how it connected to Finn's murders.

*Dusk* was a book series from the early 2000s. It had been marketed as young adult, and it was consumed mostly by teenage girls, but Finn had always been an aficionado. It was about a girl named Aurora, a witch, who was sent off to a magical boarding school where she drew the attention of vampire Cade, the son of the evil Vladimirck, and werewolf Maddox. The two teenage boys both liked her and hated each other, and the love triangle spanned the rest of the series, until the three of them graduated from Midnight Academy, and Aurora officially picked Cade.

The fanfiction *This Love* was a novel-length piece of slashfic, a term used to mean that it featured a pair of characters not paired in the original work. The word came from putting a slash between the two character's names. In this case, *This Love* was Maddox/Cade fic.

*This Love* was about Maddox and Cade accidentally killing Aurora and then bonding sexually over trying to cover up their misdeed. It was a satirical piece meant to exaggerate the ridiculous nature of love triangle tropes and to push them past that into heightened and absurd territory.

The similarities of the fic and the murders weren't anything obvious. It wasn't like *Basic Instinct* in which the killer killed in the same way as the fic. On the contrary, Aurora was killed by supernatural forces, by the vampire and werewolf being overtaken by their monstrous natures and simply going too far.

But Finn had printed out *This Love* and cut out lines from it and taped those to his victim's bodies.

It was probably macabre to analyze why.

It was probably something that shouldn't be put on YouTube.

It was certainly not what his channel and his fans wanted. They didn't like *Dusk*, for one thing, because *Hitgam* made fun of *Dusk*. And they liked television shows about vampires, not true crime. The connection was tenuous, and yet he was waist deep in an involved, in-depth series on this subject, and he couldn't stop.

He wanted to stop, just like he wanted to ease off the codeine and just like he wanted to fall asleep with the lights on.

But he couldn't.

Finn was in his head, now, all the time. He thought of *nothing* besides Finn.

He would picture Finn's face, his handsome face, that insouciant grin of his, and he would hear Finn calling him "tiger," and he would tell himself to stop thinking about that, to stop dwelling on the man that had kept him in a *cage* for months.

Thing was, he missed Finn.

Liam's hands were still shaking.

He bent down, opening the cabinet next to the sink, and he tugged out a bottle of bourbon. He debated getting a shot glass out of the cabinet above, then decided it would be a waste of water to have to wash a glass, and he went into the living room with his bourbon.

He sat down in front of his monitors, using his mouse to make his computer come to life. He was syncing audio he'd already recorded with clips from the first *Dusk* movie.

He took a pull from the bottle of bourbon.

"Here's what you're going to do, Liam," he said aloud to himself. "First, you're going to close this video, because you're not going to actually post a series of videos about Finn. You're going to dump the codeine down the toilet.

And you're definitely not going to call that cop back and tell her that you'd like to come in this evening, if it's convenient, and that you'd pay *money* to see Finn again."

He took another drink of bourbon, and he could feel the dimming feeling of the liquor begin to take the edge off of all the sharp sensations he was feeling right at that moment. Good. Nice.

He sighed and shut his eyes.

He could picture that bunker so clearly. It was if he'd never left. The dog crate hadn't been tall enough that he could stand upright, and it hadn't been long enough that he could stretch out completely. He could sit up and stretch out his legs, but if he wanted to lie down, he had to curl them up.

It was very uncomfortable.

Finn came by at least twice a day, sometimes three times. He fed him and let him go to the bathroom, but if he tried anything, Finn tased him.

Liam quickly stopped trying things. The days were long and mostly filled with boredom. He quickly began to look forward to Finn's arrival back at the bunker, if only because it was something to break up the monotony. Finn would ask him questions about how he was feeling, whether he was uncomfortable or bored or cracking up, and whatever it was that Liam said, Finn drank it in, his eyes bright.

Finn would sit down on the opposite side of the cage and drink up every aspect of Liam's suffering, savoring it like fine wine. The more Liam complained, the more Finn seemed to like it, and Liam found himself looking for things that bothered or hurt him, enumerating them in his mind in preparation to tell Finn all about it. He looked forward to that.

Now that he was released, he knew it was only because of the psychological strain he'd been under. He didn't want to be back in that dog crate, and he didn't want to suffer.

And yet…

When that cop had said that thing to him about going to see Finn, his entire body had seized up and his mouth had gotten dry. He wanted to say yes. It would be such a relief to see Finn again. It would be so good to see Finn again.

He took another drink of bourbon and then set the bottle down on his desk, next to a cluster of similar bottles, all of which were empty. Oh, wait, no. Oops. There was one with a little bit left at the bottom. He should have finished that one before opening a new one.

He rearranged the bottles, putting the half-empty one in front of the more-full one which he'd just opened.

Sucking in a breath, he shut his eyes.

He wasn't even sure why that cop had come to ask him that question. She must have known that he couldn't say yes.

The cop was kind of cute. She was a lucky one, too, with her delicate bone structure and smaller shoulders, she'd probably never have any trouble passing if she didn't have such a deep voice. Liam had dated a trans woman after college. It had been a kind of experiment on his part. He thought that someone who was transgender would fit him perfectly, someone who was a sort of mix of male and female.

But he quickly discovered it wasn't that way at all, and that Jennifer had been more female than most cis females he'd ever dated. It wasn't at all what he wanted, and Jennifer hadn't been too impressed with him either.

Of course, he'd been an ass right out of college. He had thought things like that mattered too much. The longer he dated around, the more he realized that people were people, and that very little of it mattered. Being bisexual didn't mean he was entitled to having both genders in one person. What kind of self-centered dick thought that, anyway?

Now, he was older, but, hell, maybe he was still an ass.

In terms of relationships, he was a colossal failure. His marriage with Belinda had lasted barely four years before imploding, and that had been before he'd been locked in a dog crate and had his mind twisted to the edge of sanity.

He took another pull of bourbon.

He'd wanted to say yes to the cop, but he couldn't, not without exposing his naked need for Finn's presence, and that was so fucked up that he couldn't have anyone knowing about it. Why would she have even asked? Why would the police department think that someone like him could agree to be in a room with a man who'd tortured him?

Well, they must have thought he might have said yes. He regarded the bourbon bottle, thinking it over. Yeah, they had some reason for suggesting it, but what could it have been? What had the cop said Finn wanted, anyway? To reveal the locations of bodies?

Liam set the bourbon bottle on the desk and sat up straight.

It could be as though he was doing it for the greater good, couldn't it? It would bring closure to the families of the victims. It would be a public service. He could pretend like it was difficult for him. He could say that he was doing it reluctantly.

He got up from the desk quickly and scanned the surrounding area for his cell phone.

There it was, sitting on the edge of the desk.

He snatched it up and went back to the kitchen, where the cop's card was sitting on the table. With trembling fingers, he dialed her number.

She answered after three rings. "Detective Dawson, CCPD."

"Detective," he said, and his voice was too hoarse and

too eager, "it's Liam Emerson."

"Oh, Mr. Emerson, I wasn't expecting to hear from you."

"Well, I thought it over, like you said," he replied. "I've changed my mind."

"You have?" She was surprised.

"Reluctantly," he insisted, but he wasn't sure he sounded convincing. "Only to bring closure to the victim's families. For the greater good."

"Of course," she said. "Well, that's wonderful news. We appreciate this. I know it can't be easy for you."

"No," he said. "It's difficult. Very difficult. But I'll do it anyway."

"Thank you."

"When?" His voice cracked. "When will I see him?"

"It can be arranged quickly, unless you'd rather—"

"No, let's just get in there and do it," he said, afraid he sounded too pleased at the prospect. He stumbled back into the living room and drank some more bourbon. "The sooner the better."

# CHAPTER THREE

Liam met Finn the first day he arrived at Branwen University, when he was supposed to be unpacking his mother's mini-van into his dorm room, only to discover that the dorms had been overbooked, and that—as a freshman—he had two choices.

Either live with four other guys in a student lounge on the fourth floor of Gorr Hall or move into Renwick Hall, which was the oldest dorm on campus, and which—upon seeing it—his mother had declared should be condemned and that no one should live there.

Renwick was out on the outskirts of the Branwen campus, beyond the practice football field, and a long walk from the main part of campus. The dorm's parking lot was gravel, not even paved, and it was situated a long walk from the dorm itself. There was a cracked sidewalk that wound between large trees that dripped leaves in the August heat, obscuring the building from view.

Halfway down the sidewalk, the dorm became visible. It was brick, but there were wooden balconies on the upper levels, and two wooden porches on the front and back of the building. The porches were large, like southern verandas, but the white paint on them was peeling, and they didn't look sturdy.

"No," Liam's mother said when she saw the place. "Stay in the lounge. There's a stove in there and a full-sized refrigerator. It'll be better than the regular freshman dorms, anyway. You don't want to stay in this building."

It did look grim. Liam tilted his head to the side, taking the place in. "It would be a pain to lug all my stuff down this sidewalk, I guess."

"Let's go back and say we're taking the lounge," said his mother. "They said they'd hold it for us, didn't they?"

"Come on, Mom, let's at least look inside," he said, starting forward again. Renwick was an old dorm, built sometime in the 1800s, apparently, and it had only five dorm rooms in it, two on the bottom floor and three on the top. The rooms each had their own bathrooms and kitchenettes — part of a renovation done in the 1960s when the dorm was reserved exclusively for married couples.

His mother sighed heavily. "You'll be hauling that mini-fridge on your own if you move in here, you realize that?"

"I loaded it into the car myself," he said. He had been the go-to lifter of heavy objects for the past five years of his life, since it was just him and his mom. His dad was one of those cliche deadbeats who'd disappeared in Liam's toddlerhood and had never been heard from again.

Later in his life, Liam and his father would connect on social media and Liam would spend hours looking at pictures of the man, finding the similarities in their features to be strangely mesmerizing, and wondering if he had inherited his wretched inability to form lasting attachments from the man. He and his father would send messages for three months, dancing around the idea of getting together in a restaurant and having a meal together. It would never materialize.

Liam climbed onto the porch steps, and they groaned under his weight. The wood was as rickety as it looked.

The door to the building was open and another boy filled the doorway. The other kid was tall, with large shoulders but skinny arms. He had a zit on his chin and his hair was buzzed around his head. But there was something about his eyes—this sort of infectious excitement that seemed to cut into Liam's body and light him up, as if being in the other boy's presence had suddenly taken everything to another level of existence. Liam gaped at the other boy, in awe. He felt as though he was in the presence of a celebrity or a demi-god. He was overcome.

"You moving in here?" said the boy. "You a freshman?"

Liam nodded dumbly.

"Cool," said the boy. "You know, if we go down together and say we both want to room in Renwick, we can have our pick of the rooms, they said. If we don't, they're just going to assign us roommates. There's a room on the top floor that has this nifty L-shape, and one bed could go in there and the other could go on the other side of the room, and we'd have our own spaces. You want to come see it? My name's Finn, by the way."

Liam was having trouble speaking to the god-boy. He'd never experienced this, not exactly, but it put him in mind of the time that he'd been assigned to be lab partners with Shelly Mattingly in junior year of high school. Shelley was the prettiest girl in the entire school, and she was really nice, too, so she was dazzling, too much for a mere mortal to take.

"Phineas Slater." The guy put a hand to his chest. "This your mom?"

"Yeah," said Liam.

Finn reached out, offering his hand to Liam's mother, turning a thousand-watt-white-toothed smile on her. "Nice to meet you, ma'am. What's your name?"

"Um… Maura." Was his mother blushing? She shook Finn's hand.

"If we move in together, we can help each other unpack our cars," said Finn. "Do you have a microwave, because I don't have one. I have a mini-fridge, though."

"Both," said Liam. He swallowed. "Where's the room?"

Finn's expression brightened. "Come on."

And something about that expression changed things. It was the sort of expression that people made when they shared a secret or when they were somehow on the same side. The expression made Liam feel included and accepted, and it set him at ease. His devotion to Finn was born in that moment, and it overtook him. He was falling for Phineas Slater, but he didn't know what that felt like at the time.

Liam grinned back. "Yeah, let's go look."

Finn dashed up the stairs, and Liam was right on his heels.

The room had a lot of character. The floors were dark hard wood—polished but scratched. The walls could have used an extra coat of paint. But the furniture in the rooms was the same as the furniture elsewhere. It wasn't old. There were two bunk beds and two wardrobes and two desks, even though the room had its own built-in closets. Liam could easily see how the room could be divided up so that they would each have their private areas, and he liked the kitchenette and bathroom that were attached as well. There was three times as much room in this suite than there would be in the study lounge, and he would only have to share it with one other person.

His mother arrived in the doorway of the room, looking it over appraisingly. "Well, it's big, Liam, but you have to think about the winter." She walked over to the radiator that was bolted to the wall. "An old building like this, it might lose a lot of heat. You might freeze."

"We'll buy space heaters," said Liam, running his fingers over the window sill and looking out at the view, which was nothing but trees and woods. He liked the isolation out here.

"Exactly," said Finn. "And don't worry, I'll keep my

eye on him, Maura. I'll make sure he goes to class and keeps up with his assignments. I think we'd be good roommates." He furrowed his brow. "What's your name? Did I get your name?"

Liam turned and looked Finn straight in the face. "Liam Emerson."

Finn's wide grin lit up the room. He gestured in the air as if he was looking at a billboard. "Phineas's and Liam's room."

"Yeah," said Liam, nodding. "Yeah. Let's do it."

Finn punched the air in triumph. "All right."

Liam's heart swelled. He'd never been this happy to be accepted by another human being in his life.

* * *

After hanging up with the cop, Liam downed the rest of the nearly-empty bottle of bourbon and fell asleep in his desk chair, even though it was mid-afternoon.

When he woke up to someone knocking on his door, he wished he'd managed to make it to the mattress that sprawled on the floor in his bedroom. The desk chair was comfortable enough for doing video editing, but it was murder for sleeping.

He opened the door, mouth dry, head starting to pound—had the codeine worn off so easily?—rubbing his neck.

It was his stepdaughter Madison at his door. She had a duffel bag slung over her shoulder, and her nose was red and puffy.

He stared at her in horror. "Madison, what are you doing here?" Madison was thirteen, and she was in a particularly baffling stage of girlhood, one that made her emotions so volatile that Liam was always afraid to speak to her for fear of her bursting into tears or screaming at him.

"I need to come live with you," she said.

"You need to what?" His eyes bulged.

"Let me in." She looked at him with pleading eyes.

"How did you get here?"

"I took an Uber," she said, and she ducked underneath his arm, squeezing past him and into the apartment.

"You…" He hesitated a moment, looking at the space outside the door that she had been occupying, and then he shut the door and turned to look at her.

She was staring at the living room with something like horror written all over her expression.

"Let's go into the kitchen to talk," he said.

She let her duffel drop onto the floor. "Liam? You said, and I quote, 'You don't divorce children.'"

He cringed, rubbing the back of his neck. "Well, you don't."

"You said that you wanted me to come and stay with you sometimes."

He gestured for her to go ahead of him into the kitchen.

"You said—"

"Yes," he said, going into the kitchen without her, "but then your mother told me that you said, and I quote, 'It's probably better if there's a clean break.'"

She sighed loudly.

He was in the kitchen now.

She appeared in the doorway, tossing her hair. "Well, I was confused then. It was all very traumatic for me, trying to understand what happened to you, and Mom said that you needed space, too."

"Well, something's changed your mind?" He folded his arms over his chest.

"Are you *drunk*?" She planted her hands on her hips.

"No," he said, but he said that to the floor.

She shook her head. "What the hell happened to you?"

"I don't think you should say 'hell.'"

"Oh, hell, I'm thirteen."

"Right," he said, nodding. "You're practically an adult."

"I am."

"Why are you here, Madison? Does your mother know where you are?"

Madison rolled her eyes. "I can't stand her right now." She went over to the kitchen table and flopped down in one of the chairs. "And since you two don't like each other anymore, I thought we could commiserate on how awful she is."

He sat down opposite her at the table. "Your mother is not awful."

"You're just saying that because it's some adult agreement to pretend to be on the same side against kids. But if you liked her, you two wouldn't have gotten divorced."

"It wasn't your mother's fault," he said. "It was mine."

Madison raised her eyebrows. "Did you have an affair or something?"

"No," he said.

"So, what did you do?"

"That's… the business of your mother and me. You're a kid. You don't need to worry about it."

"I thought we established that I was practically an adult."

"You have to go home."

"I want to live with you."

"No. You can't."

"Not forever, but just for a while," she said. "Just until Mom understands that if she treats me badly, I don't have to stand for it."

"I only have one bedroom," said Liam.

"But you said that I could stay with you sometimes!"

"If you hadn't wanted a clean break, I would have

gotten a two-bedroom," he said. "You have no one to blame but yourself here, Madison."

She scoffed. "You *are* drunk."

He rubbed his forehead. "We have to tell your mom where you are. But I'll ask her if you and I can go out somewhere, maybe for pizza or something. Maybe I can just bring you home in time for bed? How would that be?"

"I can't be around Mom right now, though," said Madison, her voice a squeak. "You know how she gets sometimes."

"What happened?"

"I want to go to the walking mall with Jessica."

"Your mom said no to that?" It didn't seem like an unreasonable request.

"She said she wouldn't drop me off two blocks away," said Madison. "She said she would drop me off in the parking lot, where anyone could see."

Liam raised both eyebrows.

"I can't have people *seeing me* with Mom."

Liam chuckled.

"It's not funny."

"How old do you think you appear, Madison?"

"What kind of question is that?"

"Anyone who saw you at a walking mall would assume you were driven there by someone else. You don't look old enough to drive on your own. They would just take one look at you and know you had a mother."

"Shut up, that is not true." She sat back in her chair, glowering at him.

He laughed again.

"I should have known you wouldn't understand."

"When have I ever understood you?" he said, his voice gently teasing.

"Okay, never," she admitted. She sighed. "Maybe it's fine if she drops me off. It's only... I don't know, she's in a bad mood ever since you left. Or were captured. Whatever happened."

"I did leave," he said quietly. "But then I was captured. And you know, you should cut your mother some slack. Divorces are tough."

She shrugged. "I guess so. I mean, when she and Mike got divorced, she was sad for a while. But then she met you."

"Well, maybe your mother will meet someone else."

"She says that she's cursed and that three failed marriages is a sign."

"I need to call her. You know that, right?"

Madison's shoulders slumped. "I guess."

"She's got to be worried about you."

Madison didn't say anything.

"She's probably out of her mind. She might be at the police station reporting you missing."

"You think?" Madison looked worried.

"I should probably call her right now."

"Okay, but that thing about pizza? We can still do that?"

"You don't mind being seen in public with me?"

"Well..." Madison thought about it. "I guess it's okay."

"Thanks," he said. He was dialing his phone.

"Just... tell her I don't forgive her," said Madison.

"I'll be sure to pass that along." He got up from the table and walked over to the counter, listening to the phone ring.

Belinda answered. "I can't talk to you right now. I don't know what happened to Madison."

"She's here," he said.

"Are you fucking kidding me?"

"I wouldn't do that."

A sigh on the other end. It sounded like a sob. "Why would she go to *you*?"

"I think… she's just trying to get under your skin," he said. "I wouldn't read anything into it."

"Tell her I don't forgive her!" called Madison.

"I heard that," Belinda muttered.

"I'm going to take her out for pizza and then bring her home. That okay with you?"

"Or can we go to the Thai place instead?" said Madison.

"Maybe Thai," he told Belinda. "But I'll have her home before bed."

"She has homework," said Belinda.

"Madison, your mother says you have homework," Liam said to her.

Madison rolled her eyes.

"What time should I have her back?" he said into the phone.

"By 7:00, I guess?" said Belinda.

"We can do that," said Liam. "You want to talk to her?"

"If I talk to her right now, I'm going to rip her a new one," said Belinda. "I better not."

"Okay."

"You think she's okay? I mean, going through three divorces in her young life… I've probably immeasurably fucked her up."

"She's a good kid, and you're a great mom," he said. "She's going to be fine."

On the other end of the phone, Belinda just sighed again.

He said his goodbyes and hung up with her.

Then he went to go find his keys so that he could take Madison to the Thai restaurant.

"Are you too drunk to drive?" Madison called from the kitchen.

"No," he called back. He was in the bathroom, running a wet comb through his hair. He wished he'd shaved. His straggly half-beard was not the least bit attractive. *I'll shave before I see Finn,* he thought. "I'm fine. And I'd appreciate it if you didn't tell your mother about the shape of this place."

"What do you care what she thinks of you?" said Madison.

He surveyed himself in the mirror. "I don't. But if you ever want to come back here again, she won't let you if she knows."

He rejoined her in the kitchen.

Madison was thinking this over. "Who says I even *want* to come back here?"

He shrugged. "Maybe you don't. Let's go get some Thai food."

* * *

Liam was early the day that he was supposed to meet Finn. He arrived at the prison where Finn was being kept twenty minutes early, and he sat in his car in the parking lot, anxiously scrolling through his phone, not registering anything that he was reading as he waited for the clock to tick the minutes by.

He had a new car, because his old car—a blue Nissan Cube—had been used by Finn in the murders. Finn had been attempting to frame Liam for the crimes. Liam sometimes thought that Finn had captured him because he was grooming him to actually participate in the murders. If not the killing itself, the molestation of the bodies that Finn did afterwards. Finn had wanted them to do it together.

Someone knocked on Liam's car window, and he rolled down the window.

"I thought I recognized your car," said a man standing there. He was Hispanic, with a tidy goatee and curly black hair. He was grinning. "Ricky Hernandez." He thrust his hand through the window.

Liam shook Hernandez's hand hesitantly. "Liam

Emerson."

"Oh, I know."

"Right, because you recognized my car?" Liam couldn't believe that. Also, he was a little freaked out.

"From seeing you at the station before," said Hernandez.

"The station," Liam repeated, uncomprehending.

"The police station," said Hernandez.

Liam furrowed his brow.

"Sorry," said Hernandez, laughing a little. "I observed one of your last conversations with the detectives who are building the case against Phineas Slater. They brought me in to do some investigation concerning a theory that Wren Delacroix had, that Slater wrote *This Love*."

"What?" Liam pushed his car door open.

Hernandez was forced to move out of the way of the swinging door. He laughed again.

"Sorry," said Liam, standing up, facing Hernandez. Huh. The CCPD had been holding out on him. Up until now, he'd only worked with the normal-looking officers and detectives. Now, he was apparently getting the attractive ones. First Dawson, now Hernandez.

"It's fine," said Hernandez. "I should have realized I'd startle you. I'm here to observe you and Slater today, as long as that's all right with you."

Liam's stomach sank. He should have thought of this before—that this meeting with Finn would be observed and likely recorded, and that he would be under scrutiny. His hands started to shake again. He shoved them in his pockets. "So, you're a cop?"

"Oh, no," said Hernandez. "I'm a consultant. I have a degree in popular media analysis, actually. People were always like, 'You're doing a thesis on vampire television shows? How are you going to use that later in life?' Well, joke's on them, I guess." He laughed again.

Liam didn't laugh. He tried to, but he was thinking

about the bottle of Tylenol with codeine which was in the pocket of his corduroys, and he needed one of those about now. But there was that thing that Hernandez had said. "Let's go back a minute. You think Finn wrote *This Love?*"

"I'm thinking it's likely, yes," said Hernandez. "I've spent some time analyzing a list of other fics that were written that show similarities that I think also may have been written by him as well."

Liam's hand in his pocket closed around the bottle of pills. "That fic was being posted around the same time as Finn and I were roommates in college. If he was writing it, I would have noticed. That thing is seventy thousand words long."

"You never saw him writing?"

Liam thought about it. "I guess he *could* have been writing on his laptop. I guess I didn't always pay attention to what he was doing."

"Not only did he write this fanfic, but he maintained twenty to thirty other sock puppet accounts, some of which wrote other fics and some of which created conflict and stirred up fights."

"You have proof of this?"

"Well, not exactly." Hernandez shrugged. "The IP addresses that the accounts post from are obscured, and this was all nearly twenty years ago, so it's not easy to find the proof, but I'm convinced it's true."

Liam toyed with the pill bottle in his pocket, trying to make sense of this, and trying to figure out how this information would alter the series of videos he was making about *This Love* and Finn and the murders. He'd need another video, an in-depth one, looking into all of the possible sock puppet accounts, but they shouldn't be hard to identify, because another YouTuber had actually made a video uncovering the nefarious activities of a fanfic author known as GilbertBlight, who had operated a number of sock puppet accounts and who had claimed authorship of *This Love*, amid skepticism.

"I shouldn't have blindsided you with this information," said Hernandez. "I thought you knew. Delacroix didn't tell you?"

"When we were all locked up together in the bunker, she said something about the fic once," Liam remembered. "But she didn't get into why, and I didn't press her."

"If I'd known you didn't know, I wouldn't have just come out with it like that." A troubled expression flickered across Hernandez's face. "Actually, this must be hard for you. I don't know why I'm bothering you. You probably aren't really looking forward to seeing Slater again."

"Of course I'm not," said Liam, glad his voice sounded steady when he proclaimed that.

"Of course," said Hernandez.

Liam could see that Hernandez clearly felt bad, and he didn't seem to know whether he should take his leave of Liam or stay and try to make things better. He wavered between the two, apologizing and making hints and waiting for Liam to tell him what he wanted.

Liam primarily wanted to take a pill. Or maybe two. And he wished he'd brought some bourbon, even though he shouldn't have open containers in his car. So, Liam waved Hernandez off, ducked back into his car, used a bottle of water that was warm and tepid to take his codeine, and then slumped against the headrest in the car, wishing the pills would kick in soon.

Of course, it wouldn't be that quick.

And they were going to make him sleepy as well. Maybe he shouldn't have taken them.

He debated trying to make himself throw up in the parking lot and decided that he most definitely could not do that.

Instead, he got out of the car, shut the door, and

walked with a purpose across the parking lot.

Dawson was coming from the other direction. She spotted him and gave him a little wave. She was dressed similarly to before, in a dark-colored pantsuit. Her hair was short, but long enough that it curled around her ears and the nape of her neck. She was wearing makeup.

He didn't think she'd been wearing makeup the day before, and he noted that in a puzzled way, because he'd never met a trans woman who didn't treat makeup like a competitive sport.

Maybe… maybe she was so good at makeup that the other day, she'd been able to be wearing it without looking like she was wearing it.

That was actually probably likely. Man, when he'd dated Jennifer, he'd been subjected to more conversations about makeup than he even liked to remember. His eyes would glaze over the longer she talked. Makeup was Jennifer's raison d'etre. Okay, that wasn't fair, because it made her sound shallow. He didn't mean it that way. He respected makeup as an art form, actually. It was denigrated because it was a feminine thing, but it was actually really in depth and very intricate.

Maybe it was shitty of him not to be interested.

It probably was.

He scratched the back of his head, pursing his lips.

"What?" said Dawson.

Shit. "Uh, your makeup looks good."

She touched her face self-consciously.

Shit, *shit*. He wasn't supposed to notice the makeup, right? It *was* supposed to be makeup that no one could tell she was even wearing.

"I, um, don't put it on very often," she said. "And I don't know why I put it on for a serial killer." She furrowed her brow.

"We'll be recorded, right?" said Liam. "There will be cameras?" So, she *didn't* wear makeup? Huh.

"Yeah," she said, nodding.

"You did it for the cameras," he said.

"Yeah," she said again, giving him a small smile.

He smiled back.

Now, she seemed shy.

Man, she was *really* cute. He made himself look away. What was up with him perving on everyone today? If he was bad with both Hernandez and Dawson, what was he going to be like with Finn?

He grimaced.

"Let's go in," she said, gesturing to the door.

"Sure," he said.

Right inside the door was a metal detector. Dawson went first, taking off her gun and putting it in a separate basket from her keys and badge and other various sundries. She nodded when she was told the gun would be locked up until she came back out. Weapons weren't allowed in the prison.

She went through the metal detector and nothing happened.

Liam took out his keys and wallet but not his pills. They wouldn't trip the detector, right?

They didn't, and he went through easily enough.

On the other side, Dawson led him past the reception desk. They went through another door where they were greeted by a security officer, who recognized Dawson.

"Are you bringing anything in?" he asked.

"We can't," spoke up Liam. "Can we?"

The security officer addressed him. "For situations like this, we do allow things like food or drinks to be consumed by the prisoner, as long as they're in the original packaging and haven't been opened or tampered with."

"We don't have anything like that," said Dawson to the security officer. She turned to Liam. "You're the carrot we're dangling in front of him, not some soda."

Liam sucked in a breath. There was an itch at the back of his neck. He was close to seeing Finn. Very close.

"Wait here," said the security officer. He walked down the hall. The walls were gray and the floors were gray and so were the ceilings. Once, Liam had read an article about the kinds of colors they used in both prisons and schools—muted, calming colors. In fast food restaurants, they often used brighter colors, jarring uncomfortable colors meant to subconsciously make you want to eat fast and get the fuck out. Of course, recently, they'd redone the interior of the McDonald's near him, and now all the bright reds were gone in favor of tables that were meant to look like wood grain, giving the whole place a sort of chintzy class.

Why was he thinking about fast food?

Finn had bought fast food for his victims. The theory went that he first watched them eat, then he killed them, then he raped their corpses.

Liam knew about that aspect of Finn—the voyeuristic aspect. He liked to make people give in to things, especially things they usually were too guilty to indulge in.

For Liam, that had been ecstasy.

When he was in high school, he'd had a bad run-in with the drug. He'd liked it a lot, and he'd ended up skipping school and stealing money to buy ecstasy pills. Overall, it had been a short-lived bad spot, and Liam had actually dug himself out of it. Sure, his mom had helped, but he hadn't needed an intervention or anything.

He'd woken up in the bald light of day after two weeks of bad behavior and thought, *I'm getting in over my head.*

So, he'd stopped. He'd gotten a job and paid back the money he'd stolen (mostly from his mother) and he'd never touched the stuff after that.

The minute Finn found out about Liam's history with

ecstasy, all he wanted was for the two of them to do it together. Finn pushed. Liam refused. It went on and on for six months until one Saturday night, Liam began to feel a strangely familiar good feeling. His mouth was dry. He was clenching his jaw. His body was starting to get sensitive.

Finn had drugged him. He'd gotten a pill and crushed it up and dissolved it in Liam's soda.

*It's not your fault this way,* Finn had said. *You just get to enjoy it this way. I did it as a favor to you.*

It should have been a sign. It should have made him see what Finn was. It didn't.

They'd kissed that night. That was the first time they kissed. It wouldn't be the last. No, the last was in that bunker, when he'd kissed Finn to distract him, so that he could get away from him. He still remembered the feeling of the other man's lips on his, the warmth and firmness of Finn's skin under his clothes.

The first time, it had been him kissing Finn as well. He wondered if Finn had ever initiated a kiss between the two of them. He had to have. It was only that Liam couldn't think of that now.

The security officer came back and told them to follow him.

They started down the gray hall, their feet against the gray floor.

They walked at a measured pace, and no one spoke.

They went through a security check point, waiting as the security guard swiped a card to open a massive metal door.

*What do you want?* Finn had said. *What's the one thing that you always want to do but that you can't do?*

They had been alone on one of the rickety balconies in Renwick Hall. It had been a warm spring night. The moonlight had settled like a halo on Finn's features.

Liam had been thinking about kissing him since

sometime in October when the idea first occurred to him. He had known from the moment he met Finn on that August day that they decided to be roommates that he was drawn to him, but he'd processed it like a close friendship or a kind of worship or a kind of envy.

It hadn't been for months that it had dawned on him that maybe he was attracted to Finn, like *that*.

But he pushed that thought aside, because he didn't know what to do with it. He didn't think he'd ever been attracted to another guy before Finn, and when he admitted that to Finn, his former roommate had taken it as evidence that he'd woken some latent homosexuality in Liam.

But Liam didn't believe that, not anymore. He'd examined this thought process as recently as after he'd escaped from the bunker, and he'd decided that his bisexuality had led him to simply ignore his natural attraction to men. He'd sort of assumed that it was natural, that everyone felt a bit of same-sex attraction, and that it didn't mean he wasn't straight.

Finn had twisted it all. That was what Finn did.

He shouldn't want to see this man. He shouldn't want this. *Why* did he want this?

*I can't say it out loud,* Liam had said.

*You can say anything to me.*

*No, not this.*

They had both been on ecstasy, but Finn had spent most of the time wanting to watch Liam. Watch him dance, watch him smoke cigarettes, watch him rub lotion into his own forearms. Watch, watch, watch. He'd drunk it in, his bright eyes wide, his mouth slack-jawed. The only thing that seemed to turn Finn on more was to order Liam around, to make him do things.

That was why Liam hadn't been wearing a shirt at the time. Finn had made him take it off.

The air was warm, but there was a chill on the wind.

Liam had goosebumps.

*I could show you.*

*It involves me?* Finn had been utterly gratified by that prospect.

Liam had moved forward, closing the distance between them, bringing his face inches from Finn's face, waiting, lingering, because Finn would realize what he was doing and stop him.

But their mouths touched.

Finn sucked in a breath. *Hey, look, I just want you to know, I'm not gay.*

*Me either.*

And then they were kissing again, but really kissing, tongues in each other's mouths, Finn's hands on his bare back, his bare shoulders.

In the gray hallway, the security officer came to an abrupt stop. Dawson stopped too.

Liam nearly stumbled. The pills were kicking in. He felt a wave of sleepy goodness wash through him. Good. This was what he needed. The sharp edges filed down.

If he was going to see Finn again, he needed to be a little out of it. Otherwise, it would be too much.

"Wait here," said the security officer, opening a door to their left and shutting himself inside.

Dawson looked up at him.

He met her gaze now, feeling a little fuzzy and liking it.

"Are you all right?" she said. "Say the word and we can put an end to this."

A grin split his face. "No, no. I want to do this. For the greater good." Did his voice sound slurred? Shit.

She nodded. "Good. Well, thank you."

"Sure," he said slowly. "Sure thing."

She turned away from him, peering at the door.

"Is it… is he in there?" Liam asked.

"Yes, I think so," she said.

He drew in a breath to steady himself, but his heart suddenly started to pound wildly out of rhythm. There was a wall between him and Finn. A door.

Any minute now, he was going to step through the doorway and Liam would see Finn again.

His next breath had a ragged edge.

Long moments passed.

Liam leaned against the wall, the pills taking hold. He shut his eyes. Hell, he shouldn't have taken two. The only good thing about it was that his heart seemed to be slowing down. He was feeling calmer. He could do this.

The door opened again.

Liam stood up straight.

The security officer stepped into the hallway. "We're ready for you."

# CHAPTER FOUR

Dawson did not think that Liam Emerson was fine. He didn't seem nervous, however. There was an agitation to his movements and his unsteady breath, but she couldn't quite place what it was that Liam seemed to be feeling.

And then the door opened, and they walked into the room, and she looked from Slater to Liam, and she had an odd thought.

Liam was *excited*.

Immediately, she disputed the thought. That was stupid. No one would be excited to see the person who'd kept them locked in a dog crate. That was insane.

Of course, there was Stockholm syndrome. She hadn't thought of that. Was that what was happening?

She turned to look at Phineas Slater, and for a moment, all thoughts fled from her mind.

This was the first time she'd been physically in a room with him. She'd watched videos of his interrogation, but she'd never met him. He was…

She swallowed.

Slater had a presence. She *felt* it when he looked at her. She was caught in it, as if his gaze was a net that ensnared her limbs. She could struggle, but she'd never be free, and so she didn't. She only gaped at him.

Slater wasn't the type of guy she usually found attractive. He was too coiffed, too neat. She liked men scruffier and looser. But she couldn't deny that Slater was a good-looking man. Even in his orange prison jumpsuit, even with his hair cut an inch from his skull, he looked self-possessed and handsome, and having him look her over like this, it made her feel shy and pleased.

She wanted to preen at his attention.

She forced herself not to.

Instead, she tore her gaze away from Slater and looked at Liam, who was moving across the room with a loose-limbed liquid movement, clumsy and affected, as if he was mesmerized—some mindless drone drawn to his master.

*This is a bad idea.* The thought exploded in her brain in bright, block letters, slamming almost painfully against her skull.

Liam had already sat down.

There was a table in the room, and Slater sat on one side of it. His arms were shackled. His feet were shackled. He still managed to look casual, as if he'd invited them over for dinner.

Liam sat opposite Slater, openly staring at him, his lips parted, his eyes glassy.

Hell, was he *drunk* or something?

Well, she guessed it would make sense to get a little fucked up before coming into Slater's presence. Someone should have warned her that he was like this. Maybe she should have realized it because of the way everyone in the department treated the guy. This was why he got whatever he asked for. This was why she'd been tasked with bringing Liam to him.

Shaking her head, she stalked across the room and sat down next to Liam. She leaned forward on the table, getting in between the two men, blocking Liam's sight of Slater.

"Good afternoon, Mr. Slater," she said in a businesslike voice.

Slater's eyebrows raised at the sound of her deep voice.

For the first time ever, she liked it. It was kind of nice to throw the fucker off for a second.

"I'm Detective Dawson. Let me go over the ground rules," she said. "This is not a social call, and we are not here on your agenda. You have been granted the privilege of speaking to Mr. Emerson, but he can be removed from this room at any time for any reason. I'm the person who makes that call, and it would behoove you to keep that in mind. If at any time, I feel this visit is a waste of my time or that this is in any way detrimental to Mr. Emerson, this is over. Do you understand me?"

Slater lifted his shackled hands. "Detective, are you always so… commanding?" He made it sound dirty.

She sneered at him. "Let's start talking bodies, Mr. Slater."

Slater let out a soft chuckle. He sat back in his chair and he looked past her at Liam.

Dawson glanced at Liam.

Liam's eyes were glued on Slater. His tongue darted out and he ran it over the top of his upper teeth.

"You're not looking so hot, tiger," murmured Slater.

Liam laughed, and the laugh went on too long. "You don't like it?" He spread his hands. "This is how you look on me."

"I'd take you with me if I could," Slater said. "But I can't trust you anymore. Maybe I never could."

"Bodies," said Dawson. "You were going to tell us about bodies."

Liam rubbed his neck, but he did that too slowly. Was he… caressing himself?

Oh, hell, no. Dawson needed to end this and now. Whatever the hell that was going on with Slater and Liam, it should not be allowed to continue. Definitely not.

Slater's gaze narrowed in on the place where Liam was touching himself. His breath went out of rhythm. "I want you to know I forgive you." His voice was hoarse.

"I don't forgive you," said Liam.

"We didn't have enough time together," said Slater. "It's my own fault. I brought in Delacroix and Reilly. I thought I could handle that, but it was too much, too fast. I lost control of it all. It's not your fault, what you did. You weren't ready yet."

Dawson got up. "Okay, this is going nowhere. I'm ending this. Get up, Mr. Emerson."

Liam looked up at her, eyes wide and wounded, like she'd just told him she was going to kill a puppy.

"Up," Dawson insisted, but her voice wasn't strong anymore.

"I thought you were," said Slater. "Because of Destiny."

Liam's gaze jerked back to Slater. "What's Destiny got to do with anything?"

"You know," said Slater. "You were there that night."

Liam's expression crumpled on itself. He shuddered.

Slater's smile widened. "Don't you want to talk about Destiny, tiger?"

Liam's upper lip twisted in disgust. Now, he did stand up. "I hate you." His voice cracked.

"No, you don't," said Slater.

"Let's go," said Dawson, wrapping her hand around Liam's upper arm and tugging on him. "Let's get out of here."

Liam turned to her, his motions exaggerated. He made a lurching step in response to her tugging.

It nearly threw her off balance.

So, when they went out of the door, they practically tumbled out. They ended up in the hallway, and they were both out of breath, as if they'd run a marathon.

Dawson slammed the door shut with too much force. It echoed in the gray hallway.

* * *

Liam was in the parking lot, next to his car, but he had

no memory of how he'd gotten here. Next to him, Dawson was surveying the parking lot as she put her gun back in her holster. She must be looking for her own car.

Hell, Liam wasn't sure he was going to be able to drive.

"I'm really sorry," Dawson was saying. "It's pretty obvious you should never be in the same room as that man ever again. He did a number on your head, didn't he?"

Liam felt as if he was a wrung-out wet towel, battered by the breeze as it hung to dry. Maybe that was just the codeine. He could stand a nap. He blinked at Dawson. "You, um, you have such small hands." He put his lips to his mouth, but the movement was delayed, clumsy. "Sorry. I know I shouldn't say shit like that. I'm not trying to be offensive. You're very pretty, and I don't mean to be an ass about it. It's only that you're lucky, because a lot of trans women don't have the bone structure that you have."

"I'm not..." She cocked her head to one side. "I detransitioned. I was, um, I lived as a man for over ten years, but I'm *not* a man, and I finally decided... never mind."

This astonished him. "Seriously?" Had he said she was pretty, or had he just thought that in his mind? Damn it. "I should... go." He pointed to his car.

"Of course," she said.

He turned to her. "Not because of what you said, because that's cool. I'm cool with..." He scratched above one of his eyebrows. "He *did* do a number on my head, yeah."

"He's..." She folded her arms over her chest. "I've never met anyone like that before."

"Right?" Liam laughed. "The charisma?"

"Yeah."

He reached into his pocket and took out his car keys.

He ran his fingers over the cold ridges of the one to his apartment. "How old were you when you went on T?"

She raised her eyebrows at him, probably surprised that he knew the lingo. "I started taking testosterone when I was seventeen."

"I dated a trans woman who was angry that she couldn't have gotten hormones younger, before she went through puberty. She said she always knew, for as long as she could remember, she knew she was a woman, and everyone kept expecting her to grow out of it, and she never did. She hated her voice. She got surgery on her Adam's apple. That was actually after we stopped dating. I only know because of social media." Why was he talking still? He transferred his keys to his other hand. "But, you know, I wasn't sure of fucking anything when I was a kid. Shit that I thought when I was seventeen…"

"Yeah," she said. "I'm not… I don't blame anyone except myself. It's not even a blame thing. This was a journey I was on. I needed to go through it to figure out who I was." She looked down at her shoes. "I don't usually go into this."

"Sorry," he said. "I'm sorry I pushed or said anything."

"It's okay," she said. "I appreciate that you're being… cool about it. A lot of people are secretly transphobic and they seem to want me to be, like, their vindication."

He nodded. "People have trouble with things they don't understand. Most people never thought twice about whether or not their inner identity matched their genitals. They can't empathize, and when they can't empathize, they're pretty quick to decide that can't really exist or something."

"True."

"I don't think they mean it to be as shitty as it is? Really, they should just mind their own fucking business. How the hell does it hurt them if someone they don't even know decides to transition?"

"It doesn't."

He sucked in a breath through his nose, and he turned back to look at the prison. He thought of Finn, of the way his own organs had seemed to turn to jelly in the other man's presence. He had a strange urge to start sobbing.

It was quiet, and now he noticed far-off sounds — cars traveling on a nearby road, the distant sound of birds, some muted tinny beeping noise.

"We need to go back and talk to him again," he said suddenly.

"What?" she said. "Absolutely not. He was just playing around. He didn't have any intention of telling us anything. He asked you there so he could fuck with you."

"Yeah," said Liam, squeezing his hand around the keys. "But I affected him too. And if we can find out about the bodies, we have to try."

"Can I ask you about Destiny Worth?" said Dawson.

*No.* "What do you want to know?"

"Destiny Worth is the person who owned the cabin where the bunker was kept, where you were found."

"Yes," he said. "But she's been missing since 2004."

"He killed her," said Dawson.

"Probably," said Liam.

"There was… something about it in the file, something you told Delacroix and Reilly, but nothing in your own testimony."

Liam wished she'd stop asking questions. He didn't want to *think* about this, let alone talk about it. "It's, um, it's all kind of hard to talk about."

"I realize it's delicate," she said.

"What does it matter?" He glanced at her. "It happened in Delaware. Isn't that out of your jurisdiction, too?"

"Why did he bring her up?" said Dawson.

"I don't know."

"She was your girlfriend," said Dawson. "But she was sexually involved with Slater as well?"

He rubbed his forehead. "Just that night."

"What night?"

"The last night," he said. What had he said to those detectives? He hadn't told them everything. "I walked out on her and Finn doing it, okay? And then I never saw her again. And I was very drunk that night, blackout drunk. Lots of missing time, holes in my memory. If it's not your jurisdiction, then can we drop it?"

"I'm sorry," she said. "I realize it must be difficult to talk about."

He glanced at her again. Maybe he was playing this wrong. Maybe he was going to make her suspicious, and that was the last thing he needed. "I'm sorry. I don't mean to be short with you. It *is* difficult to talk about, but if there's anything I can do to help, of course I want to do it."

"No, you don't need to apologize," she said. "I'm prying. And you haven't told me anything I didn't know from the file." She squared her shoulders. "When it comes down to it, you're right. Destiny Worth isn't our jurisdiction."

# CHAPTER FIVE

Liam met Destiny Worth outside Skelly Hall, which was the building where English classes were held. She was walking around with a pack of cigarettes, taking one out and tucking it underneath a ledge here or leaving one sitting on the arm of a bench. When Liam asked her what she was doing, she said that she was making a scavenger hunt for smokers.

"Any particular smokers?" he'd said.

"No," she said, offering him the open pack of cigarettes. "You want one?"

"I don't smoke," he said.

"Me either," she said and put a cigarette in her mouth. She got a lighter out of her pocket and lit it.

He laughed. This girl was nuts.

She took a deep drag and then started coughing. She bent over and hacked, eyes watering, and Liam didn't know what to do.

He took the cigarette from her and extinguished it in a nearby ash tray. He pounded her back.

Eventually, she stopped. "Told you I don't smoke," she said.

It was the second day of classes. He couldn't stop smiling at her. "Do you live on campus?"

"No, I have an apartment in town," she said. "Hey, you want to come over sometime? No one's come to visit me yet. I want to have, like, guests. Like we're real adults. Will you be my guest?"

"Definitely," he said.

She wasn't like any other girl he'd ever known in that he felt immediately comfortable around her. She was easy to be around, and her kookiness was infectious and fun. He went to her apartment the following afternoon, and they drank tea with maple syrup in it because she didn't have any honey or sugar, and he was awed by the size of her apartment.

She was breezy about it. "I'm one of those little rich bratty girls like in that song, 'Common People.'" She hummed it tunelessly.

He didn't place the song.

"You know," she said, starting to sing the chorus, stopping at the part about wanting to sleep with common people. She grinned at him. "I want to sleep with common people like you."

"Ah," he said, nodding. "I remember that song." It had come out five years ago, when they were younger teens.

"So," she said. "Are you game?"

"Game for what?" he said.

"Sleeping with me?"

He just laughed. How was a guy supposed to respond to that? She couldn't be serious.

She was serious.

They'd had awkward but enthusiastic sex that hadn't lasted so long that their tea got cold and then gotten dressed and went out into the small fenced-in courtyard behind her apartment to continue hanging out.

Later on that night, he left and went back to his dorm, where Finn had been waiting, wondering where the hell he'd been. Bemused, he'd said he met a girl.

"You get her number?" said Finn.

"No," said Liam. "But I know where she lives."

Except, of course, then he hadn't seen her for a week, and he hadn't gone to seek her out either. It wasn't that he hadn't thought of her from time to time, but being a freshman in college was a dizzying experience, especially living on campus. For the first time in his life, Liam had very little down time. He was always either in class or doing class work or socializing. He lost track of all his favorite TV shows. Instead, he and Finn joined a pack of freshman—there were at least twelve of them—who would all go to the dining halls together and stay up late every night talking about everything from music to philosophy to politics.

Eventually, he ran into Destiny again, back at Skelly Hall again. This time, she was expertly smoking a cigarette, and she blew smoke in his face when he greeted her.

He waved a hand in front of his face, apologetic for never having made contact since the last time he'd seen her.

She didn't seem concerned. "You want to come over again this afternoon?"

He came over.

They had more tea.

While they were drinking it, Destiny informed him that if he wanted to have sex with her again, they needed to have a conversation about female orgasms.

This should have embarrassed him. If it had been anyone else, it would have. But he found himself instead feeling grateful to have someone to talk openly about this without any pressure, because Destiny was the antithesis of pressure.

"I'm hopeless with that," he said. "Sorry. Maybe you could teach me."

She considered this and deemed it acceptable.

This became the typical pattern for them over the course of the bulk of their freshman year. They'd run into each other haphazardly somewhere and make plans to do something together. They'd meet up, do the thing, and usually have sex. Then he'd go home, and they wouldn't see each other again for weeks.

He even called her a few times. He'd gotten her number after the second encounter.

She never answered the phone when he called, and she never returned his calls.

Maybe they would have continued like that for the rest of college, but then Finn met her, and suddenly—when he'd never been before—Liam was possessive. He couldn't have given a flying fuck about Destiny's sex life up until then. He had hookups when he wasn't around her, and he figured she had them too—probably three times as many, because she was that kind of girl. None of that mattered to him.

But then, with Finn, he…

Well, anyway, after Destiny and Finn met and they were all three hanging out, it was different. He talked to her about it one day. They were in bed together in her apartment, and she was lying on her stomach, her hair splayed out over her shoulders and tangled over her face.

"Do you want to be my girlfriend?" he said. He was lying on his back, with a sheet pulled up over his crotch.

"I'm not already your girlfriend?"

He'd turned to look at her. "Well… I thought… we never talked about that."

"You want there to be rules, don't you?" she said, but she sounded eager about this, as if giving the relationship rules made it into a game. "So, are we exclusive? No fucking anyone else?"

"Obviously."

"No *kissing* anyone else?"

"Obviously." He furrowed his brow.

She giggled. "Do we get each other Valentine's gifts?"

"Uh…" He hadn't thought about this. "Well, yeah, I guess, but you have to promise not to buy expensive stuff, because I can't compete with that."

"Okay." She rolled onto her side, stretching and giving him an eyeful of her bare breasts and belly.

He reached for her.

She slapped his hand playfully. "*Anyone* else, Liam, even it's a guy."

"I'm not…" He made an annoyed face. "I wish you would stop it with the Finn and me thing. We're just friends."

"Okay," she said. "But exclusive is exclusive."

"Obviously," he said again.

And three weeks later, he was drugged on ecstasy against his will on the Renwick Hall balcony, making out with Phineas Slater.

He didn't confess his infidelity to Destiny.

* * *

By the time Dawson got home that evening, she was exhausted. The tiredness seemed to have seeped into her bones, and she felt decades older than her thirty years. She limped from her car to her front door.

The small house she was renting was too expensive, even though it was only a studio with a loft. She was six blocks from the ocean, and when she'd taken the place, there had been two rental rates—by the week and by the month. It was a vacation rental, and she was paying through the nose for it. But she was month-to-month on the lease, so she could leave any time.

It was only that she didn't want to go anywhere. She liked her little house, even if it was small. She liked the porch that stretched all the way around the place and the roof deck, where she could watch the sun rising over the water in the morning.

Lately, it was too cold, but she had spent all fall up there with her coffee, looking out over the horizon, the calmness of the morning and the endless stretch of water doing something for her soul.

She had her keys out, ready to unlock her door, when

there was movement out of the corner of her eye.

Without thinking, she pulled out her weapon and turned in the direction of the movement, baring her teeth.

"Shit!" said a familiar voice. Her ex-boyfriend Carter Simms came around the corner on the wraparound deck.

She lowered the weapon, shaking her head. "What the hell, Carter?"

"Sorry," he said. He had both of his arms up, and he looked shaken. "You're jumpy."

"I interrogated a serial killer today." She put her gun back in its holster. "You know, I gave you my address so that you could forward my mail, not so that you could randomly show up here and scare the hell out of me."

"Sorry," he said again.

She sighed. "Look, I've had a day. If there's something you need, out with it."

Carter lifted his chin. "You don't have to be a jackass about it."

"Oh my God. Are you here to call me names? Is that what we're doing?" She supposed she was lucky that they'd never gotten married. They'd talked about it enough, but she'd been the one to wriggle free of it, forced to confront her desires to wear a white dress and carry a bouquet. At first, she'd told herself that she was just experiencing some kind of latent societal pressure, that it would fade. But when they started to actually make plans for the wedding, when they got fitted for their tuxes, she couldn't handle it. She'd picked a fight with Carter and called the whole thing off, said she wasn't ready.

"No." Carter hung his head, looking chagrined. "Maybe I should come back another time."

"You could have called."

"I should have done that." He nodded. "I got in the car after work and I started driving, and then forty-five minutes later, I was here. I didn't... I wasn't really..."

She felt off-balance at that. "Why are you here?" Her voice was small.

"Uh, for some files from the Harbor that I think got mixed in with your stuff." The Harbor was a local LGBT organization where they used to volunteer. She guessed that Carter still did volunteer there. It had been a huge part of their lives. Almost all of their socializing had been connected to various events that the Harbor had put on. They'd spent nearly every evening there and most weekends too. It had been sort of their second home.

Thinking about that place and about everyone who she'd been close to there, it still made her feel like something inside her chest was being crushed.

"I don't have anything from there." She turned to the door and jammed her key inside. "I definitely don't have any files."

"Can you just check?" Carter was pleading with her. "I'll wait out here, and you can—"

"Come in," she sighed. She swung open the door and stepped inside.

Inside, there was a counter with a sink and stove tucked against the wall. A breakfast bar divided the kitchen area from the living room, which was airy and bright due to tall windows that ran up and down the walls. There was a loft area above, where her bed was. She had to climb a ladder to get up there.

But there were two bathrooms in the place—one upstairs and one down. That was luxury. It was plenty of space for her on her own.

Carter looked the place over. "This is, um, nice."

"I can't afford it." She went in and set her keys on the breakfast bar. She took off her suit jacket and her holster with her gun. She set that down next to her keys. "I'll have to leave soon. I'm looking for someplace cheaper."

Carter shifted on his feet. He clasped his hands together in front of himself and then let them go.

"I'm going to put the gun in the safe," she said. "Can't be too careful. I'll look upstairs, but I don't have any files."

Carter opened his mouth to respond, but then he hung his head, and he didn't say anything.

She climbed the ladder with her gun and pulled the safe out from under the bed. She pressed her fingerprint into the sensor, opened it, tucked her gun away, and then shut it. She looked at the stack of unpacked boxes on the far wall. She went over and opened one up. It had a bunch of books in it that she'd saved, even though she'd already read them and probably wasn't going to read them again.

"I know you don't have any files." Carter's voice filtered up from downstairs.

She closed the box and took a breath. She wanted to lie down on the bed and bury her face in the pillows, but apparently she and Carter were going to do this again. She didn't know if she could handle this again.

But, squaring her shoulders, she went back to the ladder and climbed down to face him.

He closed the distance between them. "This is stupid." He reached up tentatively. His fingers hovered inches from her face.

She shut her eyes. Some part of her wanted to lean into his touch, but she resisted it.

"You… were always… I never cared that you didn't have a… a penis, and you're still… *you*, and I—"

"Carter." Her lower lip was trembling. She shook her head. "You are a gay man."

"I know that," said Carter. "*Obviously*, I know that."

"You should be in a relationship with another man," she said.

"Yeah, but aren't we just splitting hairs about that?" He looked her over. "You don't look that different."

"Bullshit," she said. Over the years in her relationship

with Carter, she'd gone off testosterone on no fewer than three occasions, and every single time, when her facial hair started to thin out and her muscles lost definition and her body started to become curvier—when that happened, things got weird with Carter.

He always denied it. *I know you're just trying to be more natural, babe. I support you,* he would say. But he'd get moodier, weird about being with her in public, and their sex life would taper off—which he would blame on her, because going off the testosterone would lower her libido. He'd claim none of these things were happening, and that she was insecure, and that everything was fine.

Inevitably, during those periods of time, he'd start bringing up surgery. *Don't you want to go swimming without a shirt? You should look into top surgery again.*

And she would argue that she was not at all attached to her breasts—which were barely breasts anyway. She'd always been lucky to be on the smallish side. (Of course, every time she went off T, they seemed to get a little bigger, and that didn't go away when she went back on hormones, not entirely, not even if she lost a crazy amount of weight.) She *couldn't* be attached to having breasts. She was a *man*, after all, and men didn't have breasts. She would say that she was worried about the risks of losing nipple sensation and she would say it was a really expensive thing to do for vanity, basically, because she could tape her boobs down easily and she didn't care about swimming shirtless.

And then they'd fight about it, and she would get on her high horse that this was her body, and he would sulkily say that she was weird when there was estrogen in her bloodstream and…

"I miss you," said Carter, and he was touching her face.

She shut her eyes, and she tried to hold on to the memories she'd just been lost in, because it was easier when she only thought about the times he'd been dickish. It was much harder when she admitted to herself that she missed him, too.

She had met Carter when she was only four months into her transition process, and he'd flirted with her, and she'd been afraid to reciprocate, afraid to let him know that she was trans, afraid he would reject her, but he hadn't. He'd been incredibly supportive and sweet to her, and mostly, their relationship had been easy and good—like the ocean breeze.

They'd had lots of things in common. They'd both liked musical theater and they'd both been into the same kinds of music. They'd watched the same television shows and they'd been vegetarians together and then—somehow, at the same time—decided they had to go back to eating meat. They'd divided the household labor up seamlessly, with Carter cooking and doing the dishes and her doing the vacuuming and laundry.

And she remembered once, when they'd barely been together a year, and they'd been at a gay bar down near the military bases in Virginia Beach, and some older guy had started to give her a hard time, going off on trans people in some long rambling speech about how, in his day, gender had been fluid and bendable and people hadn't seen the need to go off and mutilate themselves, and he didn't hold with that sort of thing, and that gender was a social construct and she was giving it too much power over herself.

Carter had gotten in the guy's face and told him to leave his boyfriend alone, and she'd thought that Carter was going to punch the guy, and she'd never had anyone be willing to go to blows for her, and she hadn't known how to feel about it, but when they'd made love that night, she'd felt—for the first time—like they connected on this other plane, a level of transcendence that had united their souls, and she had never felt so in love with another being in her entire life.

And now, Carter was kissing her, and she kissed him back, and she made a noise in the back of her throat and ran her hand over his chest, and the kiss got deeper and more heated and—

She pulled away. "We tried," she whispered. "We tried this already."

"I want to try again," he breathed.

She took a step back, shaking her head.

"Look, I had a talk with Mindy," he said. "And she admitted that she was being shitty to say that we couldn't be part of the Harbor."

When Dawson had detransitioned, she and Carter had stayed together through it, but a contingent of people at the Harbor, led by a woman named Mindy, had decided that they were essentially a cis couple, and that they had no place in an LGBT establishment.

It had hurt Carter more than it had hurt her, of course.

Truthfully, she *was* cis now, as weird as that seemed to her.

It wasn't the loss of their connection to the Harbor that had ended their relationship. It was more than that. There were a number of things that had changed the dynamic between them. But losing the Harbor hadn't helped. It had been part of it.

She could see why he might offer it up now, as an olive branch.

But it had been months. She'd moved forty-five minutes away, to a different town, and she had a new job. Everything was different now.

"I think..." She took a deep breath. "You came up here on a whim, didn't you? This is hard for both of us. We've been together for over a decade. It's easy to want what's familiar, but—"

"Tell me you don't love me anymore," he said.

She looked down at the floor and scuffed her foot

against the carpet.

"Hayes?"

"Haysle," she supplied softly, lifting her gaze. Her first name had been spelled uniquely by her mother because her mother had wanted to honor her maiden name, Hayes. When Dawson had started her female-to-male transition, shortening it to Hayes seemed inspired.

His shoulders slumped.

"I'm sorry," she said.

"It could be a nickname," he said. "I could still call you—"

"No," she said. "You couldn't."

"You want me to go, don't you?"

"I don't," she said, and it was true. "But I've had a hell of a day, Carter, and I'm not in any emotional state right now to be making huge decisions about my life. Even if we did try to make it work, it wouldn't be easy. I have this new job now—"

"Yeah, I don't understand. How are you interrogating serial killers?" When Dawson had worked as a detective in Virginia Beach, she'd mostly hunted down stolen cars and investigated house break-ins.

"Well, I work in homicide now, and I got assigned to Phineas Slater."

"The guy who killed those prostitutes?"

"Yeah." She nodded.

"Shit." Carter ran a hand through his hair. "I don't like you doing that. You were in a room with him?"

"He was shackled. And I can take care of myself."

"Even still," said Carter. "It's not... when have you ever wanted to hunt down murderers?"

"I want to do good in the world," she said. "You know this about me. It's why I was so active in the Harbor. I need to do what I can to make the world a better place, and catching killers, that's... that's a good thing."

"That's a dangerous thing."

She shrugged.

He sighed again. "All right, I'm going to go. But can we talk again? I'll call you, and we'll set something up? Like, uh, like a date?"

She ran a hand through her hair. "I don't want to agree to anything for sure, but maybe? Call me, like you said."

"I will." He reached out, maybe to kiss her goodbye, but she shrugged away from his touch, and he looked hurt.

They dallied for a few more moments, saying goodbye, and then she finally walked him to the door and shut it behind him.

She was alone.

She crossed to the kitchen and opened the refrigerator. There was a bottle of wine on the door. She took it out and pulled the cork out. She poured herself a regular sized glass and set the bottle down. Then, she picked the bottle back up and filled the glass to the brim.

# CHAPTER SIX

When Dawson's phone started ringing at 3:00 a.m., she wished she hadn't drunk so much wine. Head pulsing painfully, she put the phone to her ear and said blearily, "Dawson."

"You're working with Slater, right?" said a male voice on the other end of the phone. "You were down here at Lowlands Correctional Facility today?"

"I was," she said, sitting up. She yawned and hoped the man on the other end couldn't hear it.

"Your boy's escaped," said the voice.

"What?" Now, she was shoving aside the covers and getting out of bed. "What do you mean?"

"There's a body," said the man. "You better get down here. We'll bring you up to speed when you arrive."

"Whose body? Did Slater kill someone? What happened?" Her heart was pounding, she realized. She was frightened.

But the person on the other end of the phone had hung up.

Dawson took the phone away from her ear and glared at it. Then she tossed it on the bed and hurriedly got dressed. She looked at herself in the mirror and her hair was a mess, so she ran it under the shower head to wet it throughly. Then she towel-dried it and combed it.

Hell, she couldn't wait for her hair to be long enough to be pulled into a ponytail. That would make things much easier.

When she arrived at the prison, she was ushered through security and brought into the cell where Slater had been kept. He'd been in isolation for his own protection, because there was concern that other prisoners might want revenge on him. Before working homicide, Slater had worked narcotics, and he'd been instrumental in bringing in a lot of people selling drugs in the area. None of them would be pleased to see him. Furthermore, in the minds of the prisoners, what they did was far less morally reprehensible than what Slater did, so they would feel vindicated if they hurt him.

No one wanted Slater killed in jail.

Everyone wanted him to stand trial for his crimes and be convicted.

If he was given the death penalty, no one would complain, of course, but it needed to be done the proper way, not with some prison shiv in the showers.

Slater had a cell to himself, and it wasn't very spacious. It contained two bunks and a toilet and sink. Everything in the cell was as gray as the rest of the prison.

Well, everything except the pool of blood that was spilling out from the back of the dead man in the middle of the floor. That wasn't gray.

The man was naked. He was lying on his back, but his legs were tucked up behind him at an angle that looked as though it would be uncomfortable if the man could feel anything anymore. His arms were splayed, and his head tilted back. He was gazing lifelessly at the upper left-hand corner of the cell.

The sight of the body made Dawson feel woozy.

Or maybe that was all the wine she'd drunk the night before.

Miraculously, she didn't seem to be having the urge to vomit. With her previous wine consumption, she thought she would. Maybe it was because the body was fresh. There was a smell, of course, the coppery smell of blood, but there was no putrescence of decomposition.

But her gaze skittered over the body and horror rose inside her, and all she wanted was to run away from this.

She'd never been to a crime scene like this before. She'd never seen a dead body, unless you counted the ones on display at viewings in funeral homes, and this wasn't anything like that.

Of course, she couldn't run away, but maybe she could take a step back. So, she did that.

"Dawson?" said someone.

She looked up and there was the security guard who'd taken her and Liam in to see Slater earlier that day.

"I'm the one who called you," he said. "I figured you'd want to know."

"Thank you," she said. Her voice was a little unsteady.

The guard didn't seem to notice. "We don't know what happened exactly, but Slater somehow lured McKenzie into the cell—"

"McKenzie is the victim?" she asked.

"Yeah, James McKenzie," said the guard. "He was a guard here. I didn't know him well. We usually worked shifts that didn't overlap much. Anyway, Slater got him in there and stabbed him in the back of the neck."

"With what?" she said. "How did he get a weapon?"

"He must have pocketed a plastic spoon at a meal and he sharpened that into a makeshift knife. He stabbed him with that. Then he took McKenzie's clothes and his key card and everything and he walked right out of here."

Her lips parted. This was incomprehensible. "No one recognized him? No one saw that it wasn't McKenzie?"

"Obviously not," said the guard.

She furrowed her brow. "Aren't there cameras?"

"The ones outside Slater's cell were disabled," said the guard. And there were no cameras inside the cells, she knew that. "They do have some footage of Slater leaving the building, but he only went through one security check, and the guys who were in there were apparently distracted and didn't even look up when he went through."

Dawson forced herself to step forward again and look into the cell. No, something wasn't right. She shook her head. "You said he stabbed McKenzie and then took his clothes?"

But the guard didn't answer. He'd been pulled aside by someone else.

"Dawson?" said another voice from behind her.

She turned. It was another detective from the CCPD, also in homicide. His name was Mitch Clark.

"I didn't know they were calling you in," said Clark.

"Well, I'm working with Slater," she said.

"Yeah, I guess so," said Clark, furrowing his brow. "But this is, you know, a murder."

"Yes, I'm aware." She blinked at him. Was he being strange or was she unable to tell anything because she was so disturbed by the sight of the body? She decided to ignore it. She gestured at McKenzie's body. "The guard took his clothes off before he was murdered. If Slater had stripped him, it would have disturbed the blood."

Clark cocked his head to one side. "Yeah, I think you're right. So, what's your theory? Slater forces him inside at knife point and forces him to strip?"

"He seduced him," said Dawson. "Maybe this wasn't even the first time. McKenzie's got to be the one who turned off the cameras outside the cell, so he was obviously anticipating that something was going to happen. It looks to me like he was maybe, um, on his knees when he was stabbed in the back of the head."

Clark grimaced.

"Look at the way he's lying," said Dawson.

"You're saying a guard was killed while he was, uh, servicing an inmate?"

"You've never met Slater, have you?"

"I worked with him for years," said Clark. "Okay, he was only in homicide for a few months, so I only worked closely with him for a while. And I knew he was gay, but he never came onto anyone that I could see."

"I'm just saying, the guy's charming," said Dawson.

"No, that's true," muttered Clark. Then his phone rang. He brought it to his ear and he answered. He gave some one-word answers, furrowing his brow. Then he hung up. "Looks like this is only the first body."

"What?" said Dawson.

"It seems as though Slater took McKenzie's car back to his house, where he killed McKenzie's girlfriend, and then he took her car. So, all our roadblocks have been looking for the wrong damned car for hours now."

Dawson swallowed. "He already killed someone else?"

"You want to head out there ahead of me?" said Clark. "I'll wrap up here and meet you there."

"Okay," said Dawson, even though she wasn't relishing the idea of another freaking body already. Two dead bodies in one night?

* * *

This body was easier, maybe because there wasn't any blood. The woman had been strangled in her bed, and it didn't look as though she'd even woken up before it had happened.

Dawson didn't understand why Slater had even bothered.

She supposed he had to come into the house to get the woman's keys, and maybe Slater had thought that it was just as easy to silence the woman permanently than to worry about her waking up while he was hunting around her house.

Still, it gave Dawson chills to think of Slater soundlessly gliding through the darkness and easing his way onto the bed to wrap his hands around the woman's throat and squeeze the life out of her. When Dawson got home, she wasn't going to be able to drift off in her bed, thinking about someone killing her in her sleep.

Fuck.

But she thought she conducted herself well at the scene, and she mentally noted what she'd say to Clark when he showed up.

But it wasn't Clark who arrived. Instead, it was Captain Moore, and he seemed astonished to see her there.

"What are you doing here?" said Moore. "I didn't authorize anyone to call you in for this."

"One of the security guards at the prison called me about McKenzie," said Dawson. "Anyway, isn't this my case? I'm working with Slater."

"You're working with Emerson," said Moore. "I thought you could convince him to help us out, because you're both members of the LGBT community."

Dawson was taken aback. Really? *This* was why she'd been assigned to this? But she wasn't any of those things. She was neither gay nor bisexual nor transgender.

And what was Liam supposed to be? Bisexual, she supposed.

"Are you all right?" said Moore. "From your previous history, I imagine you're not used to crime scenes like this."

"I'm fine," she said, lifting her chin. She didn't want to be considered weak or bad at her job.

"Well, you've done good work here," said Moore, with a patronizing smile, "but if Slater's on the loose, we don't need Emerson anymore, and we'll find you somewhere else to work."

"You'll reassign me?" she said.

"Do you enjoy this? The gore and blood? I only put you on this because of Emerson, and it seems to me, that with your strengths, we could put you to better use—"

"What if we do need Emerson?" she burst out with. She wasn't sure why she was doing this. Hell, maybe if she put another transfer in, she could go back to Virginia Beach and move back in with Carter, and maybe she'd get pregnant, and maybe everything could go back to the way it was. Maybe she was being an idiot. But part of her didn't want to let this go, especially now that Slater was on the loose. She wanted to catch that bastard and bring him back to prison. "He knows more about Slater than anyone. What if he can help us catch him?"

The captain considered this. "Well, I suppose he *has* agreed to assist us, hasn't he?"

"And I'd be good with him, like you said," she said. "We already have a relationship, and he trusts me. If you want someone to work with Emerson, it should be me."

"I guess that's true," said Moore.

"Is anyone with him right now?" she said. "Has anyone given him the news?"

"I don't think so," said Moore.

"Well, then I should probably go to him, don't you think? Maybe he can give us an idea of where we should start looking for Slater."

"All right," said the captain. "You go and see Emerson, and we'll see what shakes down from that. If it goes well, you can stay assigned to this."

"Thank you," she said, and she felt a surge of a mix of conflicting emotions. She was proud of herself, but she was frightened too. She hoped she could handle this.

* * *

Liam was asleep on his mattress in the bedroom, stacks of unpacked boxes looming over him as he slumbered. He was in a codeine-induced sleep, and when he stirred awake, it was only because someone was over him, shaking him.

Startled, he backed away from the shadowy figure,

scrambling back on the bed.

He was alight with fear, all of it zapping through him like electricity. All he could think about was running, was striking out at the thing in the room with him. He couldn't make out its features, and his brain rearranged it into something half-borne of dreams, something with too many heads and too many limbs, something that wanted to devour him with sharp, pointed teeth.

He nearly screamed, and he must have let out some kind of noise, because the thing said something.

"Calm down," came the deep register of the thing.

"Finn?" he whispered, leaning forward, crawling back over the mattress to try to see—

"It's Detective Dawson," said the voice.

He froze. "Dawson?" he breathed. Then he shook himself, and he was angry. "What are you doing in my house?"

"I knocked," she said. "I knocked a lot, and I yelled for you, and you didn't answer. I got worried. I thought that maybe Slater had gotten to you, so I came in. You should really lock your door."

He rubbed his face. "I did lock it."

"It wasn't locked."

"Why are you saying what you said about Finn getting to me?"

"Well, do you want to get up and get dressed and pull yourself together before you hear this?"

"No, I want you to tell me, right this instant." He was still angry.

"Slater escaped from prison."

Liam let out a moan. It tore itself unbidden from his lips. He leaned his head against the wall, and he shut his eyes.

"I'll, um, I'll give you a minute."

He could hear her shuffling out of the room. He wanted to pull the covers over his head and cower there.

He wanted this to be a nightmare that he could wake up from.

Instead, he got up and turned on the light. He sorted through the clothes that were lying in a pile on his floor. He thought this was the clean pile and not the dirty pile, but he did get confused sometimes. He pulled a shirt and pants on. They were wrinkled.

He went out and found that Dawson was in the kitchen, leaning against the counter. She had dark circles under her eyes, as if she hadn't slept well. He gestured for her to sit down at the table. "Tell me everything," he said.

He listened as she explained about Finn's escape, and Liam shook his head over and over again. This could not be happening. Finn was supposed to be locked up. He was in jail. He was in isolation. He wasn't supposed to simply stab a guard and waltz the hell out of there.

When he voiced something to that effect, Dawson agreed with him.

"I think he's been playing everyone," she said. "He's got a relationship with all the people at the CCPD, because they knew him when he worked there. They know he's guilty. Most of them have even seen the videos of him molesting the corpses, and yet, there's something about him, when you're in his presence, it… people need to be more careful. When we catch him again, he needs to go into a different, more secure facility, away from anyone he's ever known."

"Yeah, why didn't anyone do that to begin with?" Liam bent over and pressed his face flat into the table. It was uncomfortable, but he welcomed the discomfort. He put both of his hands on the back of his head, as if that could somehow protect him. He moaned again.

He felt Dawson's hand settle on his forearm, warm and reassuring.

He lifted his gaze.

She jerked her hand back. "Sorry. I shouldn't have…"

"It was fine," he said.

They held each other's gaze for a moment. And then another. He noticed that her eyes were green. He'd thought they were blue, but now he could see that they were a sort of green-gray color. And he was noticing that she had a little bit of dark hair growth along her jawline, traveling down like sideburns. She usually shaved it, but it was growing back. He got a strange urge to reach out and run his fingers over the stubble, to see how coarse it was.

He swallowed and he sat up, turning his gaze to the table.

"Well," she said, businesslike now, "we need to talk about where you think he might have gone."

"Oh, right," he said. "That's why you're here."

"I wanted to determine you were safe, of course," she said. "And I'll make sure that we have someone covering your house at all times. I know the captain will agree to that if it'll mean we catch Slater. Do you think he'd come here to find you?"

"I..." Liam shook his head. "I have no idea. You know, we never had any conversations about what he'd do if he escaped from prison."

"Oh," she said, clearly disappointed.

He leaned back in his chair, stifling a yawn. "Should I make us some coffee?"

She considered. "All right, sure. Thank you."

He got up and started scooping coffee into his coffee maker.

"You know him better than anyone else," she said.

He paused, mid-scoop. Could that be true? Finn didn't have much in the way of family, just a dad somewhere who didn't seem to be much interested in him, and Liam got the impression that the father had been a drunk and possibly abusive. He guessed that would fit the profile of a serial killer, wouldn't it? And Finn never seemed to keep in touch with other people from his past.

Of course, he and Finn hadn't kept in touch, either. They'd fallen out their senior year of college, and then Liam hadn't heard from Finn until he was tasing him and forcing him into the back hatch of his own car to take him to the bunker and the dog crate.

Liam dumped the coffee into the coffee maker. "He might come back for me."

"No," said Dawson, horror in her voice. "No, he said it when we went to see him yesterday. He said that he couldn't take you with him, because he couldn't trust you."

Liam turned back to face her. "Oh, yeah, I do remember that. I thought it was weird."

"Well, I completely forgot about it until this second. Some kind of detective I am. He was *telling* us that he was going to escape, and I *missed* it."

Liam filled the coffee maker with water and turned it on. "Even if we'd figured it out, we would have thought it was impossible for him to get out."

"I would have told someone to be keeping an eye on him," she said. "We could very well have prevented this and two people would still be alive. Damn it."

He sat back down at the table. "This isn't your fault."

"I need to find him," she said. "I can't let him kill anyone else. You need to help me. Where would he go?"

"I was just thinking that he doesn't really have a family," said Liam. "His mother died when he was a baby, apparently, and he would never go home to see his dad for holidays. He used to try to get me to stay in the dorms with him, but my mom missed me too much for that, so I always went home." He rubbed his forehead. "Hell, my *mom*. I need to call her."

"You think Slater would go after your family members?"

"I have no clue." Liam went to go dig up his phone.

His mother answered on the first ring, and she was horrified to learn that Finn was free. She wanted to come down there and be with him, but he couldn't bear for to see the state of his apartment, so he told her to stay put and keep her doors locked, that he was fine.

When he came back into the kitchen to pour the coffee, Dawson was getting off the phone.

"I've got someone from the department in Fairfax County looking in on your mother," she said. "Also, we're checking on your ex-wife and stepdaughter. There should be a car doing the rounds on your place all day and all night, okay?"

"Thanks," he said.

"Of course," she said.

"Let me think about where he might have gone, okay?" said Liam. "Maybe if I think it over, I'll get some kind of idea."

"All right," she said. "Maybe we could start by making some kind of list of all the places you know he liked."

"Is that where he'd go, though? Someplace he liked?"

"Or someplace where people would take care of him," she said. "He had an ex-boyfriend, I'm remembering from the file. I need to get in touch with him." She furrowed her brow. "Or do I? Am I just supposed to be working with you?"

Liam realized neither of them had touched their coffee. He got up to get some sugar and cream and spoons. He doctored his up and then sipped, hoping the coffee would kick start his brain.

"I want this," she said. "Don't get me wrong. I want to catch him. But I got to admit that I don't really have a lot of experience with this kind of thing. I've never worked homicide, let alone escaped serial killers. The captain put me on this because he thought that I'd be able to reach you, because we are both LGBT, which just goes to show his complete misunderstanding of… of everything." She took a helpless drink of her coffee.

Liam couldn't help but laugh.

She looked up at him and a laugh burst out of her too, and he could see that it was a release, that she'd needed to laugh.

Their gazes snagged on the other again.

She shook herself, turning her attention to her coffee. "I'm sorry. I don't know what's going on with me. I really didn't get much sleep, so…"

"Are you attracted to men or women?" he blurted.

She looked up at him, blushing. "I'm… Did I make you think that I…?"

"No," he said, clearing his throat, becoming interested in his own drink. "No, I'm probably projecting, and if that makes you uncomfortable, let's just pretend that I didn't even say… anything. Because I didn't really."

She laughed again.

"I'm sorry," he said. "I'm really sorry."

"Men," she said.

He looked up.

She was smiling at him.

He smiled back.

"And you?" Her voice had dropped in pitch, and he didn't know if he'd ever met anyone with a sexier voice than her. Wait, could he *unthink* that thought? Damn it. "You're bisexual?"

"Yeah," he said. "But I didn't mean to imply that I… that you…"

"No, of course not," she said. "And I didn't… because that would be unprofessional of me. Besides, my ex, he…" She took a long drink of coffee. "We should talk about Slater."

"Right," he said. Because that was all he thought about anyway. Finn. He didn't think he'd found any other person attractive since being caught and stuck in that cage. All the time he'd been out, he'd been sort of numb to everyone else, even people on TV. And then this detective, this Dawson, she seemed to have woken him up. Because he'd thought that other guy was attractive too. Hernandez, the fanfic person.

Wait, he was supposed to be thinking about Finn, not any of this.

"But you said you needed time to think," she said. "So, maybe I should leave and let you do that."

He didn't want her to leave, he found, but he thought it was best not to say that. If he was reading the situation correctly, she didn't seem to find his attraction to her offensive or uncomfortable, but she also clearly didn't want to pursue it, so he should let it alone and not make it weird for both of them. "Okay," he said. "But finish your coffee first? Maybe wait around until you know that car that's supposed to be on my house is here?"

Her mouth curved into a smile. "You need me to protect you?"

He shrugged. "You're the one with the gun and all the police training, right?"

"I am," she said, her smile widening.

* * *

Dawson went back to the station and filled out paperwork and filed reports. She checked in with the various police officers who were looking in on Liam and his family members and none of them had seen anything suspicious.

By this time, the sun was coming up.

She ducked around the corner to get some food from a fast food restaurant and then went back through Slater's file, looking for anything that might give them an idea of where to look.

She called Slater's ex-boyfriend, who hadn't seen him and seemed terrified that Slater might be coming to look for him. He requested a protective detail, and she passed that along for approval to Captain Moore.

Then she called Slater's father, who lived in Connecticut. He didn't answer the phone, so she left a message for him.

She called Liam again, but he hadn't come up with anything yet, and so she said she'd check in with him later. She drove home to her house, tired as all hell, and still suffering a bit from the effects of her wine hangover.

But as she climbed the steps to the door of her place, she was seized by a sudden concern that maybe Slater was there.

She didn't think he would come for her, but she had been there during the interrogation with Liam, and she hadn't been particularly polite to him. She'd yanked Liam out of there before Slater was done saying whatever Slater wanted to say. Maybe Slater was the type to hold a grudge.

Dawson vaguely remembered studying thrill killers when she was at the police academy, and she seemed to remember that they didn't usually kill for the same reasons as other people did. Other people might have a motive like they held a grudge and they'd lost their temper or something like that, but serial killers were motivated very differently to kill.

Even so, this was not entirely reassuring.

When she got to the stop of the steps, she walked around her wraparound porch, looking under the picnic table and pulling aside the grill to make sure he wasn't there. Finding nothing, she ascended to the roof deck.

There was nothing up there but the chair she sat on to look out at the ocean.

It was a bright and sunny day, and normally, this would have chased away any lingering fear, but she remembered what she'd seen in the woman's house earlier, and she recalled picturing Slater tiptoeing through the darkness, murder on his mind.

She gripped the railing of the roof deck and she couldn't help but picture him inside her house. He'd be wearing the guard's uniform and he'd be smiling at her like he had when he was shackled in that interview room. He'd have taken a knife out of the knife block that sat on her counter, and he'd be waiting, sitting on a stool at the breakfast bar.

*Stop this,* she told herself.

His smile would stretch on his face, too wide, so that his face was nothing but teeth, and he'd toss the knife back and forth in his hands before he leaped at her—

*No.*

She tugged out her gun, making sure it was loaded, and she held it in both hands as she carefully descended the steps from the roof deck.

On the lower deck, she made another pass, looking under the picnic table again, sticking the gun behind the grill.

Then she went to her front door.

She tried the door knob.

Locked, just as she'd left it.

That was a good sign, wasn't it?

Of course, it meant that she had to holster her gun and unlock the door, but as soon as that was done, she yanked the gun back out and nudged her door open with her foot.

She burst inside, swinging the gun in a wide arc, finger tensed on the trigger, expecting that too-toothy grin to come into view at any second.

Of course, no one was there.

She slammed the door closed, locking it again.

Her heart was beating away in her chest like a stampede of buffalo.

She checked the rest of the house.

No one was there.

But she brought the gun with her everywhere. To the

kitchen for a glass of water. To the bathroom when she had to go. And went she finally fell into bed, totally exhausted, she put it under her pillow.

Then she decided that wasn't safe. What if it accidentally went off?

She put it on the table next to the bed, sitting it right by her clock radio.

But what if Slater came in while she was sleeping and shot her in the head before she woke up?

She locked it up.

Then she got it back out again so that she could go and check the door again and make sure it was locked. She checked all the windows too.

When she slept, she dreamed of blood.

# CHAPTER SEVEN

The first time Liam saw Finn with a passed-out girl, he was a sophomore in college and he'd come home from Destiny's house instead of staying the night like he usually did because she was in one of her moods where she wanted to stay up all night and listen to music and paint.

Destiny considered herself an artist, at least sometimes. She would get into phases, and she had various obsessions during these phases. Sometimes, she painted. Other times, she would make clothing. Even other times, she would get interested in trying to learn tricks on a skateboard.

But the painting was something she always returned to. Most other things were one-offs, just something she flirted with here and there.

Her relationship with Liam was similar. She and Liam would have months-long periods of time where they'd be inseparable. They'd spend nearly every moment together, and sometimes Finn would tag along with them, but otherwise, they were each other's worlds.

And then, one day, Destiny would get interested in something else.

This new painting phase had come on quickly, and Liam wouldn't have minded it if it wasn't also accompanied by very loud music. He had class in the morning. He wanted to sleep.

But when he got back to the dorm, there was a coat

hanger on the door, which was his agreed-upon symbol with Finn that meant Finn was getting laid.

He might have kicked the door and let out a string of curse words. He must have done something, because Finn opened the door wearing only a pair of sweatpants that hung low on his hips.

Liam had seen Finn without his shirt a number of times, but something about this, knowing that Finn had been recently having sex with someone, it made Liam feel embarrassed.

Finn reached out and grasped onto Liam's shirt and pulled him into the room.

"What are you doing?" said Liam.

Finn shut the door.

The girl was lying on Finn's bed, and she was naked, and Liam remembered that her head was at a funny angle, her chin tucked against her shoulder, her eyes shut. She let out a little snore. She had small breasts that were flattened out against her chest. Her pubic hair was trimmed into a little landing strip. Her legs were wide open, and Liam could see everything.

He should have looked away. That would have been the right thing to do. But he didn't. And what was worse, his body reacted. He was aroused.

"She's really out of it," said Finn in a low voice at his ear. "She's not going to wake up. She'd never know if you wanted to screw her too."

Liam turned to look at Finn, horrified. "What the fuck, Finn?"

Finn grinned. "You could just watch me with her, then. You'd like that, wouldn't you?"

"No," said Liam. "Was she...? Did you have sex with her while she was passed out?"

Finn's grin got bigger.

"I'm leaving," Liam decided. He'd go back to Destiny and he'd try to sleep through the noise. He couldn't deal with this, with whatever this was.

"Are you saying no because of Destiny?" said Finn. "Because you know every time you two go on one of your breaks, she's spreading her shit *around*."

"No, she's not," said Liam, even though he suspected this might be true. He tried to be angry with Destiny about it, but she just wasn't *like* other people, so it was hard. She always denied it if he point-blank asked, and she got annoyed with him if he pushed at it, saying his jealousy was boring.

"She'd never know," said Finn. "No one would know except me."

Liam started for the door.

Finn caught him by the arm and pulled him into his body. He kissed Liam.

The kiss made Liam's groin pulse, and he might have groaned into Finn's mouth.

Finn's hands were suddenly everywhere. One was on the button of Liam's jeans, and whatever the hell had ever happened between him and Finn thus far, it had never been below the waist.

Liam struggled with him, breaking the kiss and pushing Finn's hands away. He was out of breath. "What the fuck, man?"

"Shh, calm down, tiger," said Finn. He propelled Liam backwards, into the wall. He kissed him again, firmly, expertly. He was rubbing Liam through his clothes.

Liam gave in to this for too long.

When Finn stopped kissing him, he didn't move his hand away. Instead, he stroked and spoke in a low, urgent voice, painting a graphic picture of the things that Liam could do to the girl on the bed, the things that he and Finn could do together, and Liam was crazy turned on and disgusted with himself.

"Stop it." Liam's voice was strangled.

"You want to," Finn murmured. "I can tell you want

to."

"I don't. I really don't." Liam wasn't sure if he was trying to convince Finn or himself.

"Liam, fuck, you're hard as hell."

Liam grunted. "Stop touching me."

Finn didn't stop. He went faster. "Is it because you're worried about the girl? You think it would hurt her somehow? She won't even know it happened. How could it hurt her?"

"Please stop." Liam bit down on his bottom lip as hard as he could. He was begging Finn, but he was doing nothing to try to get away from his roommate's touch.

"She came back here with me, and she was all about my dick," said Finn. "She wanted it, and she's not going to think it's weird to feel a little sore in the morning. She'll *never know*."

"I'll know," choked Liam.

Finn scoffed at this.

Liam opened his eyes and looked square at Finn. His voice grew stronger as he spoke. "I don't want to fuck some lifeless slab of meat that just lies there. That's not my idea of fun."

Finn let go of him, nostrils flaring. "You don't have to get like that about it."

Liam was out of breath. He gaped at Finn for a minute. Then, without a word, he flung himself out of the room and took the stairs down, his footsteps echoing noisily through the old building.

At the bottom of the steps, Timothy Rexrode was waiting for him. "Oh, it's you making all that noise. I had to know who was doing that. What's up? Where are you headed right now?"

"I..." Liam swallowed. "Nowhere." His hands were shaking. "Uh, Finn's got a girl in the room, so I'm going nowhere."

"You can crash in my bed," said Timothy. "I'm not

going to be back tonight, and Will's already asleep, so just be quiet when you let yourself in." He handed Liam his key.

"Thanks," said Liam.

"Sure," said Timothy. "Stick the key in my mailbox in the morning?" He gestured behind him at a row of numbered drawers with locks on them where the students received their mail.

"Yeah," said Liam.

When Liam got back to his room the next morning, Finn was asleep in his bed alone, and there was no sign of the girl at all.

Liam took a shower and got dressed and headed out for breakfast.

Finn was waking up, rubbing his face and yawning.

Liam decided not to say anything about what had happened between them the night before. It was all too horrible to even face, and he didn't even know what the hell he thought about it.

"Morning, tiger," said Finn.

"Morning," he said.

"Early class day?" said Finn, flopping back onto his pillow.

"Yeah," said Liam.

"See you at lunch?"

"Yeah," said Liam, and he left.

Finn didn't seem to want to talk about it either, apparently. Liam was relieved.

* * *

When the phone woke Dawson, she pulled the gun out of her safe instead of answering it.

"Fuck," she muttered, setting the gun down and looking at the phone. It was Liam calling. "Hi," she said. "Any thoughts about Slater?"

"I think we should try the obvious," said Liam.

"Which would be what?" said Dawson. "His house?

Because it went on the market as far as I'm aware."

"No, I thought the cabin," said Liam. "The place where he held me captive. Has anyone looked there?"

"We've got roadblocks on the tunnel," said Dawson. "If he went that way, we would have caught him." Of course, there was the fact that Slater had switched cars, and there had been a short period of time when they hadn't known what kind of vehicle he would be using. He could have gotten through then.

"You're positive about that?"

"Well, not a hundred percent," she admitted. "But it really *is* obvious. He wouldn't be so stupid as to go there, would he?"

"Has anyone looked there?"

"It's not technically in our jurisdiction," she said.

"No one's looked, in other words," he said.

She laughed. "We'll look, okay? But I can hardly believe it would be that easy."

"Me either, but we should start somewhere," he said.

"I'll come and pick you up," she said. "How soon can you be ready?"

"I'm ready now."

She laughed again. "Okay, well, I'm not quite there yet. I'll be there in a half hour."

* * *

"I don't know, I don't think it's about killing for him," Liam was saying. They were almost to the cabin, and he found that he was chattering too much now. He was nervous, and he couldn't seem to help himself.

At first, he and Dawson had traveled in companionable silence. She'd put on some music, and he hadn't found it objectionable, so he'd relaxed and they'd gone through the tunnel. Then they'd started heading northwest toward the mountains.

But now, they were close, and he was babbling. "I mean, I guess you know this sort of thing," Liam was saying. "I guess you studied it when you were training to be a detective."

"A little bit," she said. "If it's not about the killing, what's it about?"

"It's about the rape," he said. "I don't know when he started killing people at all, but I know he raped people on campus when we were in school and he didn't kill them, because I would see the girls afterward, and they were okay, so—"

"Wait, what?" Dawson turned away from the road to look at him.

Damn it. He hadn't mentioned that, had he? He'd confessed it to those detectives when he was locked up in the bunker with them, but somehow, no one had ever asked about it after that, and he'd decided not to bring it up, because he didn't know if he could be considered an accessory to the crimes, and he didn't think there was a statute of limitations for rape in Delaware, which was where they'd occurred, and he was a cowardly piece of shit. "He raped girls in college," he said.

"That's not in the file," said Dawson. "You never thought to mention that?"

"I..." He scrunched down in his seat and looked out the window.

"What are we talking about here?" said Dawson.

"He would drug them," said Liam. "Or maybe just get them drunk. I don't even know, because I didn't want to know. I just sometimes stumbled on it."

"On him with an unconscious woman?"

"Yeah." He licked his lips. "I mean, I should have said something back then. I knew it was wrong. I knew what he was doing was... I was horrified. I don't have any excuses. He has this way of making you feel like you're part of things."

"Part of things?"

"I didn't. I *never*..." Destiny's face swam in front of

him, her eyes dancing. *Is it good, Liam?* Bile rose in his throat. "I never *touched* one of those girls."

"I didn't accuse you of —"

"But maybe I as good as did, because I knew it was happening, and if I'd said something, he could have been stopped, and I didn't say anything. I just pretended like it never fucking happened." He clenched his hands into fists.

"How many girls?"

"How many did I see?"

"Yes."

"Three."

And then they turned onto the road that led to the cabin, and Liam's heart stuttered. It looked the same. This cabin had belonged to Destiny's family, and he and Destiny had come out here once or twice. Finn had come with them too. There hadn't been a bunker back then.

Then Finn had decided to bring his victims back to this place, but that was all part of his scheme to pin the murders on Liam. This location made Liam look more guilty than Finn, especially if the *piece de resistance* had been the discovery of Destiny's body somewhere. That would have made Liam look especially guilty.

But that had never happened. No one had found Destiny.

And this place, it didn't look as if anyone had been out here, no one from Destiny's family.

After getting free from Finn, he'd expected Destiny's family to get in touch with him, since the crime had taken place on their property, but they never had.

The theory was that the family kept things in Destiny's name for tax shelter purposes. This was probably why they'd never had her declared dead, even though she'd been missing for more than fifteen years.

Destiny's family was strange, he supposed. She had been strange, and they must have shaped her.

Dawson was saying something.

"What?" Liam said.

"Were they spread out or all at once?"

"Yeah, spread out," he said.

"So, it seems like maybe he started out with rape and then he escalated to killing," said Dawson.

"Right," said Liam. "Escalation. That's a thing." He nodded. It sounded very official, and he remembered it from serial killer documentaries.

"Rapists don't do it because of sex, you know," said Dawson.

"They do it because of power," said Liam.

"Exactly," she said.

"That's how he is," said Liam. "He has to control everything, everyone. He has to dominate it all."

Dawson stopped the car.

The cabin loomed.

Liam put his hand on his seatbelt, ready to unbuckle it, but he didn't. He let his hand linger there instead, and he stared at the cabin.

Dawson turned off the car. "It isn't your fault. You were under his influence at the time, and you were just a kid. He's the psycho, not you."

Liam nodded, but he wasn't sure if that was really true.

Dawson unbuckled her seatbelt.

Liam tried to work his, but his fingers were clumsy.

Dawson took her gun out of its holster. "Can't be too careful, of course."

Liam licked his lips. Finn could be here, he realized. He could be right here, in that cabin or inside that bunker, and if he was, they'd have to stop him.

Dawson lay her gun against her thigh and surveyed him, as if waiting for him to speak.

He only shook his head.

She watched him for a minute, and then she pushed

open the door to the car.

Liam clawed at his seatbelt, forcing it to open up. He staggered out of the car as well.

"Stay behind me," said Dawson. "We'll check the cabin first and then go down to the bunker."

Liam hadn't taken any pills or had anything to drink before this excursion. That had probably been a bad idea. He had the bottle of Tylenol with codeine in his pocket. He reached inside and let his hand close around it. Its presence was comforting.

Dawson was already halfway to the front door of the cabin.

He hurried to catch up to her. He glanced through a cluster of trees, looking out into the area behind the cabin. There was a field out there, dotted with tall trees. Somewhere out there was the trap door that led down into the bunker. He wasn't sure if he could even find it.

When Dawson arrived at the door to the cabin, she hesitated. "I need to knock and announce our presence. But I don't want to alert him to our presence if he's in the bunker. If I'm knocking and yelling out that we're here and coming in, he's going to hear."

"Isn't there, like, a rule that you can go in if you think you hear some sound of distress or something? Maybe we think we hear someone screaming."

Her lips parted. "That's lying."

"Well, maybe I'll go in and you can come after me to stop me." He tried the door. It was locked, but there was a key kept under the mat in front of the door. He peeled that aside and retrieved it and opened the door.

"You know where there's a key?" said Dawson.

"It's like I practically live here." He shrugged. "I don't think the people who own the place are going to care. They don't care about this cabin, and they don't care about Destiny." He stepped inside.

The place was sparse, with a corner containing a small

sink and a hotplate and toaster oven to round out what passed for a kitchen. There was a wood stove across the room and a bed with a quilt spread over it. It was empty inside and cold. No one was here.

He checked the bathroom quickly, pushing aside the door to make sure it was empty. The curtain over the stand-up shower was already open. The toilet had rust stains in the bowl.

There was a box of tampons sitting next to the sink, right next to a pack of toilet paper.

He furrowed his brow. What the hell was that?

"Liam, you should let me go first. I have the gun." Dawson was right behind him.

"Someone was here." Liam pointed. "But I don't think it was Finn."

Dawson went into the bathroom and picked up the pack of tampons. "Maybe he had a nosebleed."

Liam laughed wildly. "Seriously, who else would be here? No one else knows about this place."

"Maybe it's Destiny," said Dawson.

Liam didn't even respond to that. He knew that Destiny was dead. He was confused about a lot of things from that night, but he knew about that. He backed out of the bathroom and then he saw something through one of the windows—a glint of metal.

He froze.

Then he took off, tearing out of the cabin.

"Liam!" called Dawson. "Where are you going?"

He should wait for her. *Stop running,* he said to himself, but he didn't stop. He ran out behind the cabin and out past the tree that was blocking whatever had glinted through the window and there was a damned a car sitting there.

Dawson was running after him. "Liam!"

"What kind of car did McKenzie's girlfriend drive again? Was it a Honda?"

"Oh, God, you found the car?" Dawson lifted the gun. "Get behind me, damn it. Let me—" And she cut off because she tripped and fell flat on her face.

The gun went off.

Liam let out a yell of surprise, at the gunshot, at the way she'd gone down. It hadn't seemed—

She hadn't tripped.

Someone had pulled her down.

Someone who was now climbing up out of the trap door, the one that contained the bunker. Someone who was crawling over Dawson's back, reaching out with one hand for her gun.

Dawson had lost her grip on it, and she was scrabbling in the grass for it, struggling under the body on top of her, grunting.

Liam ran for them, recognizing Finn when he was only steps away.

Dawson's hand closed over the gun. And then she cried out and dropped it, and her body was shaking.

Liam heard the telltale electric sound and knew that she'd been tased.

The sound went through him and he remembered the pain and he came to a stop, unable to move his limbs.

Finn climbed over Dawson's prone form and snatched up the gun. "Hi, there, tiger."

# CHAPTER EIGHT

Dawson had been tased before, in training, and to say that it was the worst pain she'd ever experienced was not an understatement. Even now, knowing it was over, she was unable to move, struggling to catch her breath.

Well, she hadn't really thought that Slater would be here, but he was. Had he gotten the taser from the guard he'd killed? Maybe he had one stashed here. He was a former police officer, and it might be possible to claim one had been "lost," and then keep it for his own personal use.

Slater's knee was in her back. "I didn't think you'd bring the cops," he was saying. He was talking to Liam. "Maybe I should have figured that you would. I told you I couldn't bring you with me and that I couldn't trust you, but I thought you would come to me on your own. I thought…" A pause, and then Slater's knee moved away from her back. "Well, it's only a small misstep. Otherwise, everything's fine."

Dawson twisted her neck. The pain from the taser was over, but she was a little sore. Slater had her gun. He was pointing it at her, but he was looking across the field at Liam.

"What are you doing?" said Liam, who was coming closer.

"I'm going to shoot her," said Slater. "Then we can leave."

"No," said Liam.

Dawson wasn't being pinned down now. She needed to do something. She didn't think she had the strength to tackle Slater and get his gun away from him herself. She wasn't armed with her own taser—although maybe that was something to bring up with Captain Moore. Maybe she *should* have a taser.

"You don't want to come with me either?" Slater was wounded. "Why are you here?"

"I'll…" Liam's voice cracked. "I'll come with you, but don't shoot her."

"What?" Disgust laced Slater's tone. "You care about the *cop*?"

"Come on," said Liam. "Why does anyone have to get killed?"

"Killing people is the entire point," said Slater. He sighed. "I've been wanting to share this with you forever. You weren't ready when we were kids, and I tried to move on, but I never really could, so I ended up going back to it."

"To killing people," said Liam.

"Yes," said Slater. "You remember what it's like, right? That moment, right at the end, when the spark dies?"

"How would I remember?" Liam's voice shook.

Slater gestured with the gun to Dawson. "*You* could kill her."

"No," said Liam.

"It's the pinnacle experience of existence," said Slater. "You know, I think all people are wired entirely to seek pleasure. Our lives are just wandering from one search for bliss to the next. Food, sex, sleep, sherpa… all of that. But the single most pleasurable experience is the way it feels to take another human life."

Dawson wondered if she could scissor her legs around Slater's feet and knock him over that way. Should she try it, or would he shoot her if she moved?

"But even so," said Slater. "Something's been missing for me, tiger, and I tried and tried to figure out what it could be. What else should I do besides kill? And that's when I realized that it was you. *You're* what's missing. So, I went and got you, and I put you down there, and we were getting around to it, and then everything got fucked up. But I knew you'd come to me, and now we can go away together—"

"You're lying," said Liam, furrowing his brow.

"What? I think I'm monologuing," said Slater. "This is my moment of triumph, and I'm explaining myself—"

"It's about the rape. You rape them *after* you kill them. And I guess you just kill them because it's more efficient than drugging them. What happened? Did someone wake up in the middle of it, Finn? Did that really harsh on your big finish?"

Slater was quiet.

"Why are you pretending as though you like to kill things?"

Slater licked his lips. "I *do* like to kill things."

"You like to control things," said Liam. "You like to fuck things. But that thing you said… it's not you. There's something else going on here."

"There's actually a lot going on that you don't understand, tiger," said Slater. "Come with me, and I'll explain it all."

"Fine," said Liam. "But don't touch her."

Slater snorted. "You and your hard-on for trannies. You always liked boy-girls."

"Jealous?" said Liam.

Dawson decided this was her chance. She sprang out with her legs, and wrapped them around Slater's.

Slater grunted and wavered on his feet.

Dawson wrenched her legs back.

Slater went sprawling on the ground, the gun going off, the shot echoing off the sky. But he didn't lose the gun, and now he and Dawson were both on the ground.

She tried to extricate her limbs from his.

But he crawled on top of her, pressing his body into hers, putting the gun to her temple.

"Finn!" cried Liam. He was behind Slater now, yanking on the other man's hand.

Slater turned the gun on Liam. "Stop it!"

"Let her go," said Liam. "We'll tie her up. She doesn't know where we're going. She doesn't have to *die*."

"You're not ready," Slater growled. "You're just not ready yet, are you?"

Liam sneered. "You know, I guess I'm not."

Slater got to his feet. He seized Liam, pushing the gun under the other man's chin.

Liam tilted his head back, gritting his teeth.

Slater kissed Liam's cheekbone. "Not yet, then, tiger." He shot a glance at Dawson. "Car keys, if you don't mind?"

"You're going to steal a cop's car?" said Dawson. "Are you out of your mind?"

"It's not one of the ones with siren on top and the big blue letters on the side, is it?"

"Well, no, but—"

"Should suit me fine. Keys." Slater abruptly let go of Liam and trained the gun on her. "I *will* shoot you, detective. It would make Liam mad, but Liam always comes around. He and I, we have a bond, you see? *Keys*."

She glared at him, but she yanked them out of her pocket and tossed them on the ground at his feet.

Slater scooped them up and tased her again.

She screamed.

"You know that isn't how I meant for you to give me the keys," said Slater, squaring his shoulders. He turned his back on them both and loped off in the direction of where Dawson's car was parked.

Dawson struggled to her feet. She started after him,

but she wasn't quick. She was half-limping and still recovering from the taser.

Liam went to her, putting a hand on her shoulder, stopping her.

The trees had swallowed Finn up.

"I think I fucked that up," said Liam in a low voice.

In the distance, they heard the sound of a car starting.

Dawson clenched both of her hands into fists.

Liam winced.

* * *

Liam was sitting in the lobby of the Cape Christopher police station. There was a couch with plastic-covered cushions and a table with magazines that were at least fifteen years old.

Dawson had been on the phone even as Finn was driving off, and the local police had come out, followed by a bunch of people from the CCPD. They had put roadblocks up and a BOLO for Dawson's car. BOLO stood for Be On the Look Out.

The police had gone over the cabin and the bunker with a fine-toothed comb. They found the clothes that Finn had stolen from McKenzie's house after he'd killed McKenzie's girlfriend down in the bunker. Liam had declined to go down into the bunker himself. He found he didn't have the stomach for it.

Now, he and Dawson had been brought back to Cape Christopher, but Dawson had gone in to talk to the police captain right away, and Liam had been left to his own devices. He wasn't sure if he was allowed to leave or not. He didn't have his own car, but he could have gotten a Lyft or something. He wanted to go home. He wanted to attack a bottle of bourbon and fall into an alcohol-induced sleep.

However, he wasn't sure if he should. He felt as though he should stay here and wait for Dawson. He felt like this was all his own fault.

"Liam Emerson!" said a bright voice.

Liam looked up to see that Hernandez was coming across the lobby, smiling widely. Liam got to his feet.

"I want to show you something," said Hernandez, getting his phone out of his pocket. He scrolled around and then thrust the screen into Liam's hand.

Liam looked down at the phone, and the page was entirely text, rows and rows of tiny black letters that swam together. He blinked, trying to make his brain work.

And then Dawson was coming from the same place that Hernandez had come from. Her face was drawn, and she walked past him without acknowledging him.

Liam handed the phone back to Hernandez and went after Dawson. "What happened?" he called after her. "Are you in trouble? Did you blame it on me? You should blame it on me."

Dawson shot him a glance. "Not in trouble. Just the opposite."

"What's that mean?" said Liam.

Hernandez was trailing behind. "This is a new fanfic. I want you to look at it."

Dawson pushed open the door to the police station and stepped outside. It was growing dark outside, the sun setting in the west, painting the sky red and orange. "I don't think the captain really thought you were an asset, but he does now. He wants us to get together and make a list of every place we can think of that Slater would go."

"Okay," said Liam.

"I think Phineas Slater is writing this fanfic," said Hernandez, shoving the phone in front of Liam again. "Can you look at it and tell me if you think I'm right?"

"But he doesn't want us going into the field," said Dawson, who was walking into the parking lot. "He's going to work with other police departments and have them go out and check out all the spots. He thinks that's the best way to find him."

"Okay," said Liam. "So, where are you going?"

Dawson pointed at a police car—one with a siren and blue letters on the side. "I got this loaner. It's going to be a long night. I'm going to get us some food. You got any food requirements? You a vegeterian? Gluten free? Keto?"

"No, I'll eat whatever," said Liam.

She nodded and started walking again. "You're obviously a private citizen, and you can say no."

"I'm not going to say no." He was going after her again. "Hey, about what happened out there with him—"

"We don't have to talk about it." Dawson walked faster. "Sure, I'm annoyed with myself for letting him go, but it's the past. Can't change it now." She got to the car and unlocked it. She yanked open the door. "I've got us a room in the back of the station. You can wait for me there."

Liam shoved his hands in his pockets. "I guess it would be bad to ask if we could, um, drink while we were brainstorming?"

Dawson raised her eyebrows. "Drink alcohol?"

Liam bowed his head.

Hernandez shoved the phone in Liam's face again. "*Look* at it."

Liam shot the man an annoyed glance. "I'm kind of in the middle of a conversation here."

Dawson slammed the car door and started the engine.

Hernandez cocked his head to the side. "You were saying?"

Liam sighed. He took the phone.

Dawson peeled out of the parking lot, driving faster than Liam thought was warranted. All right, well, conversation over. Guess there wasn't anything to talk about, anyway.

* * *

Liam was now back in the room that Dawson had

reserved for him, waiting for her to show up with food. He was scrolling through Hernandez's phone, trying to make sense of what he was looking at. "*Bosom Friends?*"

"It just started updating today," said Hernandez.

"You think he escaped from prison and then took the time to start writing a fanfic?" Liam furrowed his brow.

"The title is a reference to *Anne of Green Gables*," said Hernandez. "GilbertBlight had a name that was a reference to that book, and he used to write trolling fanfic of that work. He would write audacious things and then have his sock puppets come in and pretend to be outraged, hoping to whip up other real readers into a similar state of outrage. He really enjoyed making people mad."

Liam furrowed his brow. "This isn't *Anne of Green Gables* fanfic, though, it's *Hitgam* fic."

"Exactly," said Hernandez. "For you."

Liam stroked his chin thoughtfully. "Okay. Maybe you're onto something here. But I don't get it. Like, is this about Frank? Because Frank is dead." Frank was a character in the show who was a witch and he'd been killed by Joe, who was a vampire. They'd been fighting over a girl. It was a takeoff on *Dusk* to some degree. Joe had gone to magic prison and then had basically disappeared from the show and the girl—Cindy—had moved on from what she called a toxic situation. The guys were given such dishwater names because they were meant to be as unappealing romantically as possible. The show was trying to make a statement about love triangles and toxic masculinity and various other issues. It was one of the reasons that *Hitgam* was considered such an intelligent show.

"Not in this alternate universe," said Hernandez. "In this universe, Frank survived, and now Joe has escaped from prison and is coming after him."

Liam felt his stomach turn over. "Well, that's a little

too on-the-nose, isn't it?"

"It's him," said Hernandez. "I really think it is."

Liam ran a hand through his hair. "Okay, okay, well… if he's Joe, and I'm Frank, and Joe and Frank are meant to be analogous to Maddox and Cade, then who's the girl? Who's Cindy or Aurora? Is that meant to be Dawson?"

"Destiny Worth," said Hernandez immediately. "Didn't you two fight over her in college or something?"

"Not exactly," said Liam. He felt ill. In *This Love*, two guys bonded sexually over murdering a girl together. That wasn't the way it had happened, but… but… hell, he'd been playing Finn's game for far too long.

"Cindy doesn't appear in this story," said Hernandez. "Well, to be honest, there are only about a thousand words up, just one chapter. Nothing much has happened except for the fact that Joe has escaped and proclaimed his desire to find Frank and finish the job."

"Finish killing him?"

Hernandez nodded.

"Great," said Liam, making a face.

"Well, he had the chance to kill you, didn't he?" Hernandez said. "I don't think he's going to kill you, because if he'd wanted to kill you, why didn't he do that when he captured you?"

"Maybe not," said Liam. "Maybe he's got something worse in mind. All right, let me look at this fic. I want to read it."

But at that moment, Dawson came in with arm loads of Chinese food. "We need to start on that list right now," she said.

Liam pushed the phone back at Hernandez. "Okay, after the list, I'm reading that fic."

# CHAPTER NINE

Finn and Destiny met each other in the spring of Liam's freshman year of college. Liam and Destiny were sitting out on the front porch of her apartment and Destiny was smoking cigarettes, something she seemed to pick up and set down much like anything else in her life, as if Destiny was like that witch in the Oz series, the one with the row of heads she kept to switch with her own — as if Destiny shed identities like a snake sheds its skin.

Though Destiny smoked occasionally, she didn't smoke inside her apartment, and she insisted on going out on the front porch to smoke. Maybe this was why she'd seemingly given it up for the winter. Too cold.

Finn was walking up the sidewalk with his backpack slung over his shoulder, looking everywhere but at the front porch, which gave Liam the impression that he'd seen him first.

In retrospect, Liam thought that maybe Finn had engineered the entire thing, following Liam here and then waiting to come into sight until Liam and Destiny were on the front porch. It was a toss-up whether they'd come out on the front porch or the back courtyard, so Liam wondered how long Finn had tried, how many times he'd followed Liam, how much he'd tried to orchestrate this.

But at the time, Liam had only seen Finn and felt a sinking sensation. He didn't want Finn to be there. What he had with Destiny was his only real respite from Finn. He lived with Finn. He ate every meal with Finn. Finn was everywhere, all the time, except when Liam was with Destiny, and he didn't want Finn to be here now.

So, Liam sat there and pretended not to recognize Finn and hoped that Finn would somehow miraculously walk by without seeing them or turn the corner and walk back towards campus. It seemed odd to Liam that Finn would be out here randomly, three blocks away from any campus buildings, but the truth was that the walk from Destiny's apartment to class was shorter than from Renwick Hall.

Finn kept coming and kept looking at his feet or occasionally up at the sky, and Liam kept waiting, hoping... He held his breath and licked his lips, and Destiny said, "Why do you keep looking at that guy?"

Liam turned to her, cursing himself inwardly, and said, "I think that might be my roommate."

Finn was close enough to be in earshot, of course, and he turned his gaze on Liam, smiling a wide, knowing grin, as if he knew Liam was uncomfortable and he enjoyed it. "Liam? What are you doing out here?"

"It *is* you," said Liam lamely.

"Is that the girl I hear so much about?" said Finn, turning to Destiny. "Destiny?"

"That's me," said Destiny, stubbing out her cigarette in an ashtray. "It's funny, because I don't know your name."

"What? Really? Doesn't Liam talk about me?" said Finn.

"Never," said Destiny. She glanced at Liam, and she also seemed to be enjoying this. "What's your name?"

Finn climbed onto the porch with the two of them. He offered Destiny his hand and focused his entire being on her. "Phineas Slater."

Liam knew exactly what it was like when Finn turned on the charm, and he didn't like him doing it to Destiny, because Destiny already seemed less than interested in

Liam, and he couldn't bear the thought of losing the both of them.

He *would* lose them, he knew, if they ended up with each other, because it would be too painful to watch the two of them together. It would smash his heart into shards.

"Phineas," said Destiny, as if she was tasting the word, moving it around in her mouth and deciding whether or not she wanted to say it again. They shook hands.

"You can call me Finn," said Finn. He kept his eyes on her. "Right, tiger?"

"Yeah," said Liam quietly.

Destiny turned to look at Liam.

Finn's gaze followed hers.

Now, Finn and Liam were looking directly at each other. Finn's eyes were wounded and luminous. Liam could read the questions there. *Why did you hide me from her? Why did you pretend not to see me? Aren't we friends? Aren't we* best *friends?*

Destiny laughed. "Oh, holy fuck. Kiss already, you two." She lit another cigarette.

Finn yanked his gaze away from Liam's to look at Destiny. "What did you just say?"

Destiny held out her pack of cigarettes. "I said you should kiss. The sexual tension, hell, it's thick. You want a smoke?"

Finn didn't smoke, but he took a cigarette and put it in his mouth. "I'm not gay."

"Right," said Destiny, reaching out with her lighter and flicking it.

Finn leaned into the flame and lit his cigarette, inhaling. "Neither is Liam."

Liam swallowed. "Yeah, I'm definitely not… gay."

"Okay, okay, whatever. You guys are repressed." Destiny snickered. "Would you kiss if I was there, in the middle of it? We could do it now. You guys make out and I'll watch."

Finn decided this was a joke and laughed. "She's exactly like you said, Liam."

"What did he say about me?" said Destiny.

"That you say whatever crosses your mind," said Finn, sucking thoughtfully on his cigarette. "I'm figure it's going to be more like you and Liam are making out and I'm watching, though. Third wheel, reporting for duty."

Destiny laughed. "Oh, poor Phineas. Liam's abandoned you, and you're jealous. Well, I will be sure to include you." She grinned at him. But then she scampered over to Liam and snatched him by the chin and kissed him hard, thrusting her tongue into his mouth.

Liam made a muffled sound of protest, especially because he could tell that Destiny was keeping her gaze on Finn the whole time she was kissing him.

Finn brought the cigarette to his lips and took a drag. The smoke came out with his words. "I'm really happy to have met you, Destiny."

* * *

"Well," Dawson said, coming back into the room. It was after midnight, and she'd been summoned to find out some news about the list they'd turned over to other police departments. "Apparently Renwick Hall is condemned. There was a fire there a few years back, and they never repaired the place. It's boarded up and empty. Nothing there."

Liam groaned. "Figures." The list, such as it was, hadn't been too great, but he'd listed every place that had been significant to him and Finn throughout their college career, even the original bunker, but the police officers from Delaware who'd been sent out to look into it hadn't found it. He was probably going to have to go find it himself.

"So, I think that's everything on the list," she said.

105

"All checked out, and nothing."

"Most of it is in Delaware," said Liam. "How many hours' drive is that? He wouldn't even be there yet."

"Right," said Dawson. "So, people are waiting, watching, and if he shows up, we'll nab him. I think we should probably go to bed."

Liam nodded. "I guess so. But, um, if this doesn't shake out, if there's nothing in any of the places on my list, then what?"

"We'll have to try something else," said Dawson. She started to gather up the empty Chinese food containers. "Did Hernandez go home?"

"Nah, he's just in the bathroom," said Liam. "But I'll go find him and tell him we're packing it in." He'd like to go home and have at least a little bourbon before bed. Even though he was incredibly tired, he didn't think he could sleep without it. That and the codeine, of course. He got up from the table, stretching.

The door to the room burst open, and Hernandez was there, waving his phone. "He posted a new chapter."

"On *Bosom Friends*?" said Liam. "I haven't even read the first chapter."

"Joe leaves a bouquet of cut-off limbs on Frank's doorstep," said Hernandez. "There's a note that reads, 'Let's dance.' Frank uses witchcraft to determine that the limbs belong to Cindy, and he puts them in a magical stasis and goes to the ballroom at Rowan University, where he finds Cindy, barely alive, and magically reattaches her legs and arms."

"That's disturbing," said Dawson. "What is this, anyway?"

"We think that Finn is posting this fic," said Liam. "It's a message for me."

"Yeah, like a coded message," said Hernandez. "What do you think it means?"

"Is there some way to trace where he's posting this

from?" said Dawson. "Like an IP address or something?"

"He's cloaking the IP," said Hernandez. "I kicked it over the IT guys the minute I saw it, and they told me it's untraceable."

"Figures we couldn't catch a break." Dawson sighed. "Okay, well, who's Frank?"

Hernandez started explaining to her. Then Liam jumped in to elucidate some other point that Hernandez had made. Then Hernandez jumped in to explain further.

"Stop," said Dawson. "This is… okay, you two, if it's a coded message, can you crack the code?"

"I think it's obvious that he's back at Branwen University," said Hernandez.

"Which is good, because we've got people scoping out every place that has any significance to the two of you," said Dawson.

Liam scratched the side of his jaw. "How long is this chapter?"

"About two thousand words."

Liam considered. "I write scripts for my YouTube videos, and sometimes they're really long, like eight thousand to ten thousand words. I almost never write them all in one sitting. I feel like it might take two hours to write that much. Maybe less, but at least an hour. And he can't take any of the typical routes to get there, because we set up roadblocks within twenty minutes of him leaving the cabin. So, he has to be taking some circuitous route, and there's just not enough time for him to have driven there and written this thing."

"So, you don't think he's in Delaware?"

"What if he wrote this in prison?" said Hernandez.

"He'd still have to type it," said Liam.

"And he doesn't have enough time to drive to Delaware and type this out?" said Dawson.

"I think he might have enough time," said Hernandez.

Liam gripped the back of the seat where he'd been

sitting. "Once, Finn and Destiny and me came all the way down to this rave outside of Richmond. It was in a warehouse, and we all danced together. And the note says, 'Let's dance.'"

"Okay," said Dawson. "Good. So, let's find the address and we'll get someone out there right away."

Liam took a deep breath. "No."

"No?" said Dawson.

"I want to go," said Liam.

She sighed.

"Don't you want to go?" said Liam. "Don't you want to confront him again?"

Dawson wouldn't meet his gaze.

"I don't want to confront him," spoke up Hernandez. "Just for the record? I'm good with never being in the same room with him."

Dawson lifted her head, smiling. "Understood, Hernandez."

"So?" said Liam.

"What are you saying?" she said. "You're going to refuse to give us the address unless we say you can come along?"

"The captain said that you weren't any good in the field, right?" said Liam. "He values you because you can work with me, but otherwise he doesn't think you're a very good cop."

"We should have had backup when we went to the cabin," said Dawson.

"Fine, sure," said Liam. "Backup. Let's bring some people with us. But I can't sit here in this room waiting. It's driving me insane."

Dawson tapped her fingers on the table. "Well... technically, the captain is asleep right now, and maybe this is the kind of thing where we should beg for forgiveness instead of asking for permission?"

"Exactly," said Liam. "Think of it. If we bring Finn in

this time, the captain will have to eat his words about you. You'll have proved yourself."

"Right," said Dawson. "So, let me go and see if I can get a couple of uniforms to come with us, and we'll head out to this warehouse. Near Richmond, you say, so an hour and a half away?"

"On the other side, actually," said Liam. "Probably a little less than an hour from here."

"Good," said Dawson, taking a deep breath.

* * *

Dawson hadn't made friends at work, exactly, but she was friendly enough with a few of the other female police officers and when she explained to them that Moore had essentially removed her from her own case and said that she shouldn't go into the field, all three of them agreed it was time to show Moore how wrong he was about them.

One of them, named Amy Brice, said that Moore meant well, but he could be a sexist bastard sometimes. "He just thinks the guys need to take care of us. Well, he's wrong about that."

So, they all set out for the warehouse.

When they arrived, it was after 2:00 a.m., and they pulled into the empty parking lot to look at the old square building squatting there in the darkness.

Liam told them that it was even more run-down that it had been when he was in college, which had been more than fifteen years ago, so that wasn't surprising.

The doors to the place were hanging off their hinges, swinging a bit in a chilly breeze. They made a clanging noise that seemed to dully echo through the building and the empty lot.

Dawson had to admit that this was all a little creepy, but she forced the thought from her head. She couldn't afford to let this place give her the heebie-jeebies and screw everything up.

They pushed through the doors, the armed women

going first and Liam bringing up the rear.

Inside, there was one big, empty room, but it was full of stacks of wooden pallets, some so high that they almost reached the tall ceiling.

"Whoa," whispered Liam. "It wasn't like this before. There was nothing in here at all. Except, you know, sweaty dancing bodies."

"We'll check the pallet stacks out," said Dawson. "Carefully, we look behind each one. I'll go first." She turned to the other officers. "You guys cover me."

The others nodded.

Dawson started toward the first stack of pallets, moving stealthily, holding up her weapon. When she reached it, she eased herself around the stack, and then jerked to the other side.

Something moved.

Dawson followed the movement with her gun.

It was a rat—huge thing—too big to exist, she thought. Its whiplike tail dragged across the concrete. She panted. She'd almost shot it. Damn.

"Yuck," said Brice. "Anything but rats."

"Seriously," agreed Liam.

One of the other officers let out a nervous laugh of relief.

Immediately, from somewhere in the warehouse, there was an answering laugh.

They all froze.

The laugh went on and on. It was high-pitched and wild, like a cartoon villain. It sent chills up Dawson's spine. Her palms started to sweat, and she tightened her grip on her gun.

"Where is that coming from?" muttered Brice.

"Split up," said Dawson, gesturing with her gun. "You two to the sides, and Brice and I will take the middle."

"I'm with you," said Liam, moving behind her.

Dawson didn't dispute this. She darted forward, not worrying about being quiet now. She and Liam ran for another stack of pallets.

They went around it. Nothing was there.

Dawson looked around, pointing her gun in all the corners and shadows.

There was nothing.

She started for the next pile of pallets.

A gun shot echoed through the warehouse.

A female voice screamed.

# CHAPTER TEN

Dawson swerved around the pallets, sprinting now, gun in both hands in front of her. It was dark, and she could barely make out anything in front of her. Her heart had begun to beat too fast and out of rhythm, and it seemed to her that her breath was the loudest thing in the entire universe.

Movement.

Something streaking towards her.

Dawson skidded to a stop, tightening her grip on her gun, sucking in three noisy breaths in quick succession.

It was a person. The person had a gun, and the person fired.

Dawson hit the floor, sweeping her leg out behind her as she did so. Her leg collided with Liam's shins, and he went down too, grunting.

Dawson's shoulder made impact with the cold concrete floor, and it hurt.

But she ignored that, lifting the gun and leveling it. She squeezed off a shot at the person coming for them. Now, she could see it was a woman—her hair in a sloppy braid that swung behind her as she ran for them.

Dawson's gun shot cracked through the air.

The woman halted mid-movement, hit by the bullet. She swung her arm around wildly, getting off another shot before she crumpled to the ground.

Dawson cringed, but she was all right. She turned to Liam, whose eyes were wide and whose breathing was noisy too. "Hurt?" she gasped.

He shook his head.

Dawson turned back to the crumpled form of the woman on the floor. She waited for movement. She'd taken the woman down, but the woman had still been able to shoot. Dawson needed to get the gun from that woman.

She began to crawl across the floor.

From the left, Brice appeared.

"Stay there!" Dawson called to her, not wanting the woman to shoot again.

Brice halted.

The downed woman didn't stir at the noise.

Dawson hesitated. "Drop your weapon," she ordered.

Nothing from the motionless form on the floor.

Dawson pushed herself to her feet. Slowly, she moved across the room, covering the downed woman with her gun the entire time.

No movement.

Nothing.

She stepped over the woman, aiming her gun at the woman's throat.

The woman's eyes were wide open. Her face was dirty. There was blood. Dawson couldn't see the gun.

She began to kneel to look for it.

The woman's arm shot up, flinging the barrel of her weapon into Dawson's face.

Dawson had her gun on the woman as well. She should have shot already, shot again, but now she had to weigh whether or not the woman could get her shot off first. And would Dawson be able to incapacitate the woman before she hurt others?

Dawson bared her teeth. "Drop it," she growled.

The woman let out a high-pitched laugh, and Dawson knew she was the source of the laughter before. It was the same laugh.

"The highest form of love is sacrifice," said the woman. "The highest form of success is sacrifice. I will be one with the all-seeing eye." Then, too quick, she turned the gun on herself, fitting the barrel of the gun beneath her chin. The gunshot was loud, and her head jerked back, and blood sprayed out behind her unraveling braid.

# CHAPTER ELEVEN

They searched the entire warehouse after that, and by the time they found the bouquet of arms and legs in the back corner, more cops had arrived, because — of course — they'd had to call in the dead body.

The macabre tangle of flesh and bone was tied together with a red ribbon and had baby's breath tucked in between the fingers and toes. Liam saw it and thought he was going to lose all the Chinese food they'd eaten earlier.

The scene was photographed and processed, and everything was transferred back to the crime lab.

Liam didn't vomit.

He really wished he had some bourbon though. He would have downed one of his codeine pills if he hadn't been afraid that he would fall asleep on his feet. It had been a long time since he'd slept, and by the time they returned to the station in Cape Christopher, the sun was coming up.

He and Dawson talked about the woman, because none of that made any sense.

Who was the woman? What had she been doing there? Why had she shot herself and tried to shoot them?

Dawson thought that maybe she was a victim of Finn, but that didn't really make any sense, because she'd been left there alone, with a weapon. Why wouldn't she have left the scene once she was alone? Why would he give one of his victims a gun?

So, then there was the idea that maybe Finn was working with this woman, that she was part of it. But that seemed odd as well. There was no indication that Finn had a partner in crime. But it did make more sense for her to shoot herself if she knew she was guilty.

Then there were all the strange things that she'd said about sacrifice and love and success and the all-seeing eye. What the heck was that?

All in all, it wouldn't even seem connected to Finn if it weren't for finding the severed limb bouquet, just like the fanfic. Could the woman have just happened to be there? Some crazy homeless woman already squatting in the warehouse when Finn arrived? Maybe she'd even already had the gun. Maybe Finn had left her there to screw with their heads.

As for the bouquet itself, it was frozen, or at least it had been. It had been thawing, but some of the fingers and toes still had ice crystals on them. So that would indicate difficulty in determining the time of death for the bodies to which the limbs belonged. They could have been on ice for years.

To Liam, this only meant one thing. These were Destiny's body parts. No wonder no one had ever found her body. Finn had been keeping her in a freezer somewhere for all these years. For her part, Dawson seemed to agree with him, but she was also a little bit concerned about how Moore was going to react to what had happened. He'd specifically ordered them not to go into the field, and she had shot someone.

Would he blame them for the fact that the Jane Doe she had shot was now dead, or would he be pleased that they'd recovered so much more evidence?

Liam said he'd wait with her until she spoke to Moore, but Dawson told him that wasn't necessary, and she told him to go home.

Liam wanted to wait until they got some identity on

the limbs. He wanted confirmation that they belonged to Destiny. But Dawson informed him that wouldn't be easily forthcoming. It took days, possibly weeks, for DNA results to come back. Furthermore, without a sample of Destiny's DNA to test against, they couldn't confirm it was her.

So, he left and went home.

He sat down at his computer, looked at the video he was in the middle of editing, and wondered when he'd get back to it. He took a pill and chased it with some bourbon.

Belatedly, he worried that Finn was somewhere in the house and went on a search of the place, which didn't take too long, since his apartment was not very large. He uncovered nothing.

He drank until everything was fuzzy, and he didn't have an image of Destiny's face continuing to appear behind his lids every time he closed them, until he didn't think about Destiny's bare skin.

He drank until everything blurred into everything else and oblivion claimed him.

* * *

Dawson was in the middle of talking to people in the lab when Moore summoned her to his office. In the lab, they'd been telling her that the arms didn't belong to the same woman—that it was one arm from one victim and one arm from another victim, and that one of the arms didn't seem to have been frozen as long, which they could tell because of the lack of ice crystals on it. In other words, it wasn't freezer burned.

They also thought the legs belonged to different victims as well.

So, unlike the fanfic, in which the bouquet belonged to Cindy—the Destiny analogue—this bouquet belonged to at least two different victims, assuming the arms and legs matched, but probably three, because of the difference in

117

freezing time for one of the arms, and maybe as many as four. They couldn't be sure about that yet, since they were just going off of observation at this point.

Dawson was puzzling this through as she knocked on the door to Moore's office.

He had just arrived for the morning and he had a large takeout cup of coffee that he was drinking. He set that down on the desk and told her to close the door.

She did.

"Did I not make it clear that I wanted you with Emerson?" said Moore.

"I've been with Emerson," she said. "Well, I just sent him home to get some shuteye, but otherwise, we've been together."

"So, you took him out to the scene then?" said Moore.

She nodded. "I did."

Moore rubbed his chin. "Even so, I told you that I wanted you two to be working on ideas and that we'd send other officers out to investigate, didn't I?"

"You did," she said. She clasped her hands behind her back and surveyed him. She wasn't going to offer excuses, and she wasn't going to apologize. That wasn't her way.

"But you directly disobeyed my orders."

"Yes."

He sighed.

She waited.

"Were you offended that I told you to stand down? Was that it?" he said.

"Offended, sir?"

"You had something to prove?" he said, taking a drink of coffee. "I suppose you'll tell me that when you lived as a man, you were treated differently."

She stifled a smile. "Well, I was. But I also never worked a case quite like this. I will admit that when Liam and I went to investigate at the cabin, it was a bad idea not to take backup, and so this time, I did bring other officers."

"Yes, but you were the one who handled the Jane Doe," he said. "Brice tells me you didn't hesitate, and that you were cool-headed and efficient in the face of danger. She was impressed."

Dawson hadn't expected that.

Moore set his coffee down on the table. "Maybe I was a little unfair to you, Dawson. I won't bench you from here on out if you promise not to disobey my orders. Do we have a deal?"

She nodded. "Yes, sir."

"Good," said Moore. "Now, I need *you* to go home and get some shuteye, because this thing is just getting weirder and weirder, and I need you fresh on it."

"But I just came from the lab, and—"

"And you know as well as I do that it'll be days—maybe even a week—before we have anything from a DNA test, so you might as well go home and sleep."

She took a deep breath. "All right."

"Good," said Moore. "Dismissed, then."

* * *

Dawson awoke to the sound of the phone ringing.

Something else must have happened with the case. She fumbled for her phone, but it wasn't ringing.

That was when she realized it was her personal phone ringing, not her work phone. She found that instead and saw that it was Carter calling. She answered.

"Hey," said Carter.

"Hey," she said. "Look, I know I told you to call me, but the thing is, I'm really involved in this case right now, and I don't know if I have the brain power to focus on other stuff, like *us* stuff, so maybe if I could call you when things are a little less crazy?"

"This is the serial killer case?" he said.

"Yeah," she said.

"Man, why don't you just ask to be transferred off

that?"

She sat up straight in bed. "Why would you say that?"

"That's not even your thing. You've never been interested in homicide. You used to say that people glamorized it because of TV shows, but that in real life it would just get in your head and screw you up."

"Did I say that?" Maybe she vaguely remembered saying that, but she thought she might have been at a party, and maybe she'd said it because people always thought that if she was a police detective it meant she solved murders, and that got old.

"You don't need to be screwed up. I bet you're already having nightmares. Or, hell, you're going to have to shoot someone someday."

"Actually…" She didn't finish the sentence. Even though her shot had only wounded the Jane Doe, not killed her, it was the first time she'd ever discharged her weapon in the line of duty. She would have thought such a thing would unnerve her. But oddly, she found she had no real reaction to it, other than extreme curiosity about the Jane Doe.

She felt entirely justified in having shot the woman. The Jane Doe had fired two shots on them, and she'd clearly intended them harm. She was obviously out of her mind and dangerous. Dawson'd had no choice but to do what she did, and she didn't feel screwed-up over it at all. It was funny, but in the moment, everything had seemed clear. She'd been in a heightened state, but she hadn't been panicked. Instead, she'd felt clear-headed and calm. She was actually proud of herself for handling it all so well.

"Actually, what?"

"I don't want to be transferred off the case," she said. "I think I might be kind of good at this."

"At serial killers? Are you kidding me? That's not you."

"You know what, Carter, I'm not sure you ever knew me."

He made a noise of indignant disbelief on the other end of the phone.

"It wasn't your fault," she said hurriedly. "It was my fault. I didn't know myself either. I didn't want to know myself. All I wanted to do was to keep the status quo. Any time I questioned anything about myself, I shoved it down. I was afraid to know myself. How could you have known me if I didn't know myself?"

"So, what? You're saying that everything we had together was a lie or something?"

She was quiet.

"That's bullshit, Hayes. You loved me, and I loved you, and—"

"Haysle," she said quietly.

"Oh, for fuck's sake." He was annoyed. "Don't be like that about it."

"If I were transitioning to male from female, you'd just apologize. You'd respect me."

"That's not fair," he said. "After everything we had together—"

"Well, like you just said, what we had together was a lie."

There was only stunned silence on the other end of the phone.

"Listen, I'm sorry. I did say that I'm not really able to focus on all this right now, didn't I?"

"That really freaking hurts," he muttered.

"I don't mean it..." She sighed. "I'm sorry. I was a coward. I was afraid, because I had tried something to fix myself, and it hadn't worked, but I *wanted* it to have worked, you know? I really wanted to be fixed. I needed to lie to both of us, because otherwise, I was going to have to face that fact that I was broken and that there was no way to fix me at all. I couldn't face that."

"*Do* you feel broken?"

She sighed. "Everyone's broken, Carter."

"I'm not."

"Okay, well, good for you, then." She rolled her eyes.

"I mean, if I am, it's only because when you left, you broke my heart, and I haven't gotten over that."

"I'm sorry," she said softly.

"I feel sometimes like I'm missing a limb or something, you know? I don't feel whole."

"I'm not your missing arm, Carter." She rolled her eyes again. "I'm a complete person, and you're a complete person, and neither of us need the other to function."

"It's a metaphor," he said.

"I'm going to need to call you back," she said.

"What?"

"Sorry," she said. "I just… I thought of something, and it's important, and I'll call you back, okay?" She hung up.

* * *

Dawson burst into the lab, pushing open the door to the room where she knew that they had the pieces of the bouquet laid out to be analyzed.

"Dawson," said Anthony Frisk, who was standing over a severed leg with a hair dryer. "I thought you got sent home to sleep."

"Two months ago," said Dawson, "there was a body recovered of a sex worker who was out near the ocean, right? Do you remember what I'm talking about?"

Frisk furrowed his brow. "Um, we get a lot of dead sex workers in this lab unfortunately. Was this one of Slater's victims?"

"No, it was assumed she might have succumbed to the elements," said Dawson.

Frisk's eyes lit up. "I remember this! The woman who they thought got stuck out in that strip of foliage and growth that runs up and down the coast? She had drugs in her system, and she was out of it, and they thought she got stuck in the marsh and died?"

"Yes," said Dawson.

"She was missing an arm," said Frisk, punching the air.

"Yes!" said Dawson. "You took fingerprints, right?"

"Yes," said Frisk. "Wait here. There's a computer connected to the fingerprint database in the other room. Let me run a quick analysis. Do not move." He took off at a jog out of the room, leaving the hair dryer sitting out on the metal slab, still running.

Dawson didn't move. She squinted at the hair dryer.

Time passed.

Dawson shifted on her feet.

Frisk was back, with a printout. "Boom! Yes, the fingerprints on the newer arm, it's her."

Dawson grinned at him. "It is?"

"Yes," he said. "We'll have an expert look over the computer results, just in case, of course, but the analysis is rarely wrong."

"So, she was found not too far from Slater's burial site, so… this is connected. He took her arm."

"Well, it was cut off post mortem," said Frisk. "We thought an animal got it. It was kind of ripped off."

"She got away from him," said Dawson. "He was trying to kill her, but she got away from him. She ran around in those trees and bushes and got stuck in the marsh and couldn't get free. By the time he found her, she was too dead and too gross to rape, so he took her arm."

"Could be," said Frisk. "I don't do that part. I just analyze the bodies."

She furrowed her brow. "That's weird, isn't it? I don't know a lot about serial killers, but I don't think they usually evolve into taking trophies. Honestly, since Slater escaped from prison, it's like he's playing with a new playbook or something. What the hell is going on?"

"I think that's your job," said Frisk, winking at her. "But this is huge, identifying these victims. Now, if we just had something to go on for the others."

"I guess you fingerprinted them. Can you check them against the database?" She considered. "I guess I could do that. Can you show me how? That's something I haven't gotten any instruction on. New on the job here."

"Sure," said Frisk. "This way." He started towards the door. "Oh, that Destiny Worth person had been fingerprinted because she was a student teacher, and they're required to have fingerprints on file. So, if you don't find a match, you'll know that the other arm isn't hers. We won't know about the legs, of course."

"We'd have to wait on DNA," said Dawson.

"And unless we have a sample from Destiny Worth to test it against, we won't know," said Frisk.

Dawson nodded. She couldn't be sure, but she thought Liam's theory was wrong. She didn't think any of these body parts were going to be from Destiny Worth.

Frisk showed her how to use her personal login to get into the fingerprint database and how to call up any prints that had already been scanned into the system.

She called up the fingerprints in the database for Destiny Worth and had the computer check them against the ones for the arm.

"You got this?" said Frisk.

"Yeah, I'm good," she said. "Thanks."

He gave her a nod and left her to it.

Dawson's phone rang. Not her work phone, but her personal phone. Damn it, she had meant to turn that off. She usually did when she was at the station.

Well, maybe she wasn't technically back on the job. There was no one else around, so she answered it.

"Carter, I can't talk right now. I'm at work. I'll call you back," she said.

"No, it's fine," said Carter. "I think you were right before, anyway. This is over. I have to stop clinging to this."

She waited to feel something at that, but there was nothing.

Carter was still talking. "It's only that I don't understand. You and I, we had a mission. We were going to make the world better for gay people and better for trans people. Everything we did was about that. And how do you abandon that?"

"Well, I'm not gay or trans anymore," she said, looking across the room at the window, where the last of the evening sunlight was spilling tiredly into the room.

"Why does that matter? Aren't those issues still important?"

"They are, and I still support them," she said. "But it's not right for me to take the spotlight away from people who are gay and trans in favor of me. And because of my story, I can even be detrimental to it all. People want to look at me as some confirmation that being cis is the only thing that's right, that I just turned back to 'normal.' So, it can't be my fight anymore. You have to see that."

"Maybe," he said in a quiet voice.

"This… what I'm doing here, at the station, with this case… I think *this* is my fight," she said.

"Seriously?" A long pause, and when he spoke again, he was whispering. "Maybe you're right. Maybe I never did really know you."

"I'm sorry." She was whispering too.

It was quiet.

"Carter," she murmured. "I did love you. What we had together, it was real."

"I know," he said. "But it's over now."

"It is," she said.

On the screen, the analysis had finished. No match. The severed arm did not belong to Destiny Worth.

# CHAPTER TWELVE

Liam woke up, and it was dark outside. He had slept the whole day away, but he guessed that was warranted, considering that he had been awake the entire night. He checked his phone, thinking he must have missed some communication from Dawson, but there was nothing.

Well, maybe they didn't need him. It was apparently going to take some time to identify the limbs in the bouquet, and when they did, he wasn't sure how he was going to feel about it all.

He couldn't help feeling a niggling sense of worry, but certainly there couldn't be any real evidence to be found on her arms and legs, especially if they'd been frozen for all these years.

He would be better trying to get something else done, on his videos, for instance.

Right now, his income was holding steady, because his other videos were still pulling in ad revenue and because of his patrons on Patreon. He could probably wait some time before he'd notice any wavering in that area, but if he didn't put out any new content for too long, then he might lose some patrons. And the YouTube algorithm seemed to favor regular output, of course. If he had one video doing well, then YouTube would recommend others of his videos to people watching. A rising tide lifted all boats.

So, there was every reason to get back to work.

And yet, he found himself checking to see if there was

a new chapter on *Bosom Friends* instead. There wasn't.

He'd just woken up, but it was late in the day, so he decided it was a perfect time for bourbon. He cracked open one of his bottles and started to drink. He thought about Finn. He thought about the cage. He thought about Destiny.

No.

*Think about anything but Destiny,* he told himself.

Finally, he called Dawson.

"Do you need anything from me?" he said. "Do we know anything new?"

She brought him up to speed on what they'd discovered about the limbs. They didn't all belong to one person. One arm belonged to a woman who'd been discovered two months ago. The others probably belonged to two other victims. One of them might be Destiny.

But maybe none of them were Destiny.

This cheered him for some reason. Maybe they'd never find Destiny's body, and they'd never ask any questions about it. Worse things could happen.

He found he was able to turn back to his work on his YouTube videos, and now that he had more information about Finn and it was practically confirmed that Finn had written *This Love*, he had a lot of fodder to expand his series of videos. He knew that it wasn't strictly within the purview of his brand, but he thought that it was a hot enough idea that it might help him branch out and find an even bigger audience.

He was excited.

He worked late into the night and fell asleep in the wee hours of the morning.

When he woke up, it was too early, and his phone was ringing.

It was Dawson.

"The captain is hoping you'll want to continue to

assist us," she said.

"Of course I do," said Liam. His mouth was dry. He'd probably put away another bottle of bourbon the night before.

"Well, do you think you can come down to the station, then?" she said. "He says it'll be easier if he talks to both of us at once."

"I'll be there," he said.

* * *

Liam had taken a half of a Tylenol with codeine to dull the headache that he had raging behind his temples. He thought that maybe half a pill wouldn't make him so sleepy. He was yawning, though, as he settled down in a chair in front of Captain Moore's desk in the captain's office.

Dawson was already seated next to him, sitting up straight, staring at the captain. She was wearing a pair of tiny gold earrings. They were shaped like seahorses.

Liam wasn't sure why he fixated on that detail, but he liked that part of her face, he supposed. He liked her delicate bone structure and her small, feminine ear and the way it was juxtaposed against the area of her face she obviously still had to shave. There was a teensy bit of stubble there, and he wanted to run his thumb over it in the worst way.

"Mr. Emerson?" prompted Moore.

"Hmm?" Liam's gaze snapped up to the captain.

"I said that we appreciate your cooperation with the investigation," said Moore. "Please, do let us know if we're interfering with your day-to-day activities."

"I'm flexible," said Liam. "Besides, I really want to catch Finn."

Moore gave him a nod.

Liam had met this man originally when he'd been brought in after escaping with Delacroix and Reilly from the bunker. They'd separated him from the federal agents and put him in another interrogation room, where they'd asked him tons of questions. Moore himself had taken a turn, coming in to grill him.

At the time, Liam had gotten the impression that they didn't believe his testimony. After all, Finn did work for the department. They all liked him. Liam knew just how likable Finn could be.

But then they'd found the video evidence of Finn and the corpses, and their treatment of him changed utterly. Suddenly, he was an important eye witness that they needed to take care of, not a possible suspect in multiple grisly murders.

Moore was talking again. "Well, I'm not asking for nothing here. I know that I had indicated before that I wanted your contribution to only be of intelligence, and that I didn't want either Dawson or you out in the field anymore. But I've reconsidered that position, and I think you could both be valuable. However, Mr. Emerson, if you don't wish to travel, I'd understand."

"Wait, we're talking about travel?" said Liam. "To where?"

"To Delaware, to Branwen University," said Moore. "There's been a run-in with Slater there."

Dawson managed to sit up even straighter. "There has? What happened?"

"He managed to get hold of one of the officers that was trying to bring him in," said Moore. "Used the man as a shield. Took him hostage. Now, they have no idea where he might be, and they haven't heard anything from Slater."

"Where'd they find him?"

"Well, they were looking in the places you indicated," said Moore. "So, that's why they were able to make contact at all. I understand that this took place outside a dorm building. It's condemned and abandoned now, but I suppose it's where you lived with Slater?"

"Renwick Hall," said Liam. "They found him outside Renwick Hall."

"Anyway, the local department there is very eager for your assistance," said Moore. "So, if you would be so good as to head up there, maybe we could actually catch this guy and bring him in before he kills anyone else."

"Absolutely," said Liam. "When do we leave?"

"As soon as possible," said Moore. "Detective Dawson, is this all right with you?"

"Of course, sir," said Dawson. "Whatever it takes to bring this guy in."

"Excellent," said Moore. "Thank you both very much."

* * *

The drive up to Delaware took over four hours, and they arrived sometime in the afternoon. They were met at Renwick Hall by a detective named Melanie Householder. It was her partner who'd been taking hostage. His name was Jim Kaveney, and Householder was grim as she took them through what had happened.

Householder and Kaveney had approached the abandoned building that had once been Renwick Hall, and Finn had been underneath the fallen-down porch.

Liam was stunned to see what shape Renwick was in. It had never looked very good from the outside, but the building was now dilapidated. There was graffiti all over the outer walls, which had been damaged and stained by smoke. Part of the roof had been burned away, and the windows were boarded up. The front porch had collapsed. It was like a child's stack of blocks—knocked over and forgotten, gathering dust in the corner of a toy room.

Householder continued explaining what had happened. She said that Finn had hurtled out towards them, unheeding when Kaveney called out for him to halt.

They hadn't even been able to identify him, considering that he was running at them at top speed.

The two officers had drawn their weapons but hesitated. Householder expressed regret at not shooting Finn, but Liam didn't think cops should go around shooting people just because they ran at them, so he understood why she hadn't. If they'd been able to identify him, it would have made sense, he supposed.

He tried not to be relieved that Finn wasn't shot dead. He shouldn't want Finn to live.

*I don't want him to live,* he thought, but it didn't even sound convincing in his head.

Kaveney had tried to subdue Finn using his baton, but Finn used his taser, and Kaveney went down.

Then Finn had took Kaveney's gun—though he must still have had Dawson's somewhere as well—and he'd used that to threaten Kaveney and get Householder to drop her weapon as well.

Householder delivered all of this information to them with a bowed head. She clearly blamed herself. She should have shot Finn, she said, when he was running at them, but she had allowed Kaveney—who was about a decade more experienced than she was—to take the lead, and she had followed him.

Dawson reassured her, saying that one couldn't be too careful with a person's life, and that Kaveney's caution meant he was a good cop. She said she respected him.

But Householder *wasn't* reassured by this. Finn could see on her face that she was convinced Kaveney was already dead and that she held herself personally responsible for this fact.

"I guess we'd been lulled into a false sense of security, since we'd found nothing at any of the other places we checked," said Householder. "We shouldn't have let our guard down, but we did."

"You had no idea that he would really be here," said

Dawson. "There was nothing to say that he'd come to Delaware. Last sighting had been in Virginia, and his car hadn't been seen on any of the normal routes."

"Even so," said Householder.

Dawson put a hand on the other police officer's shoulder. "Blaming yourself doesn't help anyone."

Householder didn't answer, but Liam thought she would always blame herself, and he understood the feeling. It made him wish for a drink of bourbon or another half of a codeine pill. He put his hands into his pockets to feel around for the container of pills, but he only clutched it. He didn't take it out.

Dawson's car had been recovered as well. It had been parked behind the building.

Householder berated herself for not noticing the tracks in the tall grass, but Liam didn't think they were noticeable unless you knew to be looking for them.

Dawson couldn't have her car back, of course, because it was in the local impound, and it was evidence.

Householder wanted to know where Finn might have taken Kaveney.

Liam said that he didn't know any places besides the ones he'd already submitted to the department, the places they'd been checking when they found Finn in the first place.

"What about the bunker?" said Liam.

"There's nothing there," said Householder. "That field you're talking about, the one behind the practice football field? It's been paved over and turned into a parking lot."

"Oh," said Liam. "Really? Then I guess the bunker's gone. He wouldn't be there."

"There's nowhere else you spent any time?" said Dawson.

"Nowhere," said Liam.

"So, besides the dorm, and those bars, and the bunker, you were never anywhere else?" said Dawson.

"The park down by the river," said Liam.

"We've looked there thoroughly," said Householder.

"Including the woods surrounding it?"

"I suppose we could look again," said Householder.

"What about Destiny Worth? Did she live in this dorm too?"

"No, she had an apartment in town," said Liam. "We did spend time there, of course, but I'm sure it's rented out to someone else now."

"We should check that out anyway," said Householder.

Liam gave her the address.

* * *

Dawson decided they'd drive out to the apartment, so she had Liam direct her, and drove out and parked across the street from the place.

There were several cars parked out front, but no one answered the door when they knocked. She called Householder about that, who said she'd already been by, and got no answer, and that she was in the process of getting a warrant to go inside.

Dawson relayed the information to Liam, who was incredulous that they thought anyone in that apartment could have anything to do with the case. He also seemed badly affected when they were near it. Dawson thought that the death of Destiny Worth had deeply scarred the man. She felt for him. It seemed that Liam Emerson had been through too much.

Maybe they shouldn't have him out here in the field. Maybe it was all too much for him.

However, she couldn't help but feel strangely energized by everything. She told Householder they'd like to be there when the warrant was served, and then she and Liam went to find a hotel so that they could settle in for the night.

They got adjoining rooms and she left him to go to

133

hers.

Once she'd unzipped her suitcase and changed out of her suit into a pair of jeans, she began to think about dinner. Should she and Liam eat together or should they just order in room service?

There was a knock at the adjoining door, and she went to open it.

Liam took in her jeans and sweater, and a small smile stole over his face.

She felt her cheeks heat up, and she scolded herself. Liam was wounded and severely screwed up. He had some strange thing for a serial killer. She could still remember that he had readily agreed to going away with Slater, something she'd never spoken to Liam about. Liam would probably claim he was just playing along with the other man, but she knew better. She'd seen the way they looked at each other.

No, Liam was bad news in every way, and it didn't make any sense to be blushing.

"I was, uh, thinking about dinner," said Liam.

"Yeah," she said. "Me too."

"So, if I asked you to eat with me, you'd say?" His smile widened.

"Well, the CCPD would be paying for it, so it's not like it would be a…" *Don't say date, Haysle.*

"We're professional collaborators, detective," he said in an amused voice. "I wouldn't dare suggest otherwise."

"No, there's nothing to… to suggest." She was smoothing out her sweater too much. Sweaters didn't even get wrinkled for God's sake.

"There's a restaurant attached to the hotel," said Liam. "Downstairs."

"Right," she said. "We could do that. We'll, um, talk about the case."

"Okay," he said. Why was his smile even bigger?

"Okay," she said, trying not to smile herself, and

failing.

They stared at each other again, both smiling, and she didn't know what the hell was wrong with her.

When they got there and got settled in a booth in the corner, he ordered an alcoholic drink. She figured that they were in walking distance of their room, and that she was off duty, and what the hell? She ordered one too. The restaurant was a steakhouse. They both ordered steaks.

They waited a bit and then their drink orders arrived. As the drink worked its way into her system, she felt looser, and he seemed to as well.

He started volunteering things. "Finn has this thing about watching people eat," Liam said. "He liked to go out to a restaurant and order all the appetizers on the menu and then encourage people to try each and every one of them. He'd stare at you while you ate. You'd think it would be creepy, but it wasn't. It always made me feel sort of warm and easy and good."

"I read about that," she said. "That he would take his victims out for fast food before he killed them."

"Right," said Liam.

"Can I ask you something?" she asked.

"You can ask," he said. "I can't guarantee I'll answer."

"Fair enough," she said. "Why's he call you 'tiger'?"

Liam made a face. "It started as a joke, and it really got under my skin, so he kept doing it. After a while, I guess I got used to it."

"Sorry," she said.

He shrugged. "You could have asked me a much worse question. I thought you were going to."

"Like why he said the two of you have a bond?"

Liam looked at his plate.

"I'm not asking that," she said quickly. "I don't need to know."

"We weren't… involved," said Liam. "Not really, anyway. He was never my boyfriend or anything official like that, and anything that did happen was always this weird, shameful secret thing that we never talked about, because we were both taking a pretty intense no-homo stance about everything. It was the early 2000s, and I was a confused kid."

"Oh, believe me, I understand all about being a confused kid," she said.

He chuckled. "I bet you do."

She took a drink of her cocktail and grinned at him. Normally, someone saying that would rankle in some way, but she didn't feel that from Liam. She wasn't sure why, but it was probably also a bad sign. An even worse sign was that she suddenly felt like talking about her transition, and she never wanted to talk about it. "It didn't start when I was a kid," she said. "I mean, it did, it obviously did, but I never felt like a, um, like a boy when I was a little kid. I guess I was kind of a tomboy. I wasn't particularly thrilled with frills and pink, but I wore dresses. I played with Barbies."

"Yeah?" He was looking at her with eager eyes, drinking her in, and she was reminded of the way he looked at Slater. He was looking at her that same way.

Her stomach turned over. "I don't even know why I'm telling you this. I hate talking about this."

"You don't have to tell me," he said.

"Okay," she said. She took a drink of her cocktail.

"You *can* tell me, of course. I'd be lying if I said I wasn't curious. But I don't mean to pry, and I don't want you to feel uncomfortable."

Her fingers wandered idly over the napkin-wrapped silverware in front of her. "It's only that talking about it always makes me sound insane, and no one ever understands. It's an insane thing to do, change your gender."

"I don't know." He shrugged. "I think everyone wonders about it. I bet lots of people even fantasize about what it would be like to be the opposite gender."

"Yeah," she agreed.

"It's not the same, of course."

"No," she said.

He took a drink of his drink.

She started to unwrap her silverware.

"Should I change the subject?"

"No," she said, smoothing out the napkin, running her fingers over the fork.

But at that point, they were interrupted when the server brought out their food.

They spent several moments buttering their potatoes, sprinkling pepper, and pouring steak sauce, and when he spoke again, she almost felt startled.

"Maybe I could take a guess about it all, and you could tell me where I get it wrong?" he said.

She tilted her head to one side, considering. "All right, fine."

He picked up his steak knife. "Well, I imagine you were an adolescent, probably fifteen or sixteen, when you first found out about transitioning, and you probably stumbled across a lot of first-person testimonies from transgender people who'd had great experiences with it. They probably told stories about how, their whole life, they'd felt wrong is some unfathomable way, and then, when their bodies changed, all that was fixed, and they were suddenly right and whole and happy."

She nodded. "Actually, yes. I found a forum online, full of transgender people, and there were threads following the transition processes for all of them."

He cut his steak. "Maybe you'd never felt, your whole life, that you were a man, but you *had* felt wrong."

"Yes," she said. "Like I didn't fit. And especially amongst women. It's like… I don't know… other women are all taught some strange girl-language at birth and they all communicate with each other wordlessly about all manner of things, and I always did things wrong with other girls. I could never understand them."

He chuckled.

"Well, as an example? You know how when a girl tells you that you're not supposed to tell anyone something, that it's a secret?"

He nodded slowly.

"That's not really what's meant," she said. "You *are* allowed to tell some people, if you trust those people, and if you're certain they won't spread it around. You can always tell your boyfriend, for instance? And usually your best female friend, not that I ever had one of those."

Liam furrowed his brow. "I don't think that's the way it is. I think that women are just shit at keeping secrets."

"No, no, there is an unspoken code and all other women understand it except me. I don't get these things. They are intuitive to other women, but to me…" She sat back in the booth, still feeling frustrated about this.

Liam was amused. He put steak in his mouth and chewed.

"I didn't start taking hormones because of that, of course."

He swallowed. "Not *just* because of that."

"I think maybe I might have been undiagnosed, but I might have a very mild form of autism," she said. "It's why I'm socially awkward, and why I'm literal about some things, and it's what was wrong with me all along. Not my gender, after all."

"That makes a lot of sense, actually," said Liam, taking a drink of his cocktail. "I can see all that."

"Well, I can't be sure. I take those autism diagnosis tests and sometimes I pass and sometimes I fail. I guess it doesn't matter in the end. What matters is that the transitioning didn't work for me."

"You tried it," he said, "and instead of feeling as though everything was fixed, and that you were whole and happy, you felt just as wrong as ever."

"Yes," she said. "I was still wrong. And now I was sort of… a freak."

"No." He shook his head. "Never a freak."

She ducked her head down, embarrassed, because there was that look in his eyes again.

"You could never be anything other than…" He trailed off, and then he picked up his drink. "Sorry. I'm sorry." He took a drink.

She gazed at him, her lips parted, and they just looked at each other for a while. Finally, heat rising in her cheeks, she picked up her cocktail and took a big gulp. "Don't be sorry." Her voice sounded different. Unsteady.

He ran his tongue over his bottom lip.

She picked up her fork and began sawing at her steak. "Anyway, I felt as though I'd gone too far, and that I couldn't go back. I was…" She touched her neck. "I had an Adam's apple. I was growing hair all over my face and my body. My voice…"

"I love your voice," he murmured. "Your voice is incredibly sexy."

Her breath caught in her throat.

He winced. "I didn't say that."

"Thank you," she whispered.

He gave her a small smile. "You're welcome."

She smiled too.

"So…" His voice was soft. "Even though you still felt wrong, you didn't detransition, but you didn't go any further either? No surgeries, nothing like that."

"I just… couldn't," she said. "But at the same time… I don't know. Things were good. I had a boyfriend, and I was in love with him, and we were happy. I didn't want to screw everything up."

"I get that," he said. "I understand that."

"When I dreamed," she said, "I was always female. It was like, deep down, I knew that this wasn't right. But…"

"So, what finally made you decide to detransition? Did you and your boyfriend break up?"

"No," she said. "The opposite, actually. We wanted to have children."

"Ah," he said, looking into his drink.

"We looked into adoption, but… it seemed stupidly expensive and needlessly difficult when I had, you know, a *womb*."

"So, you went off the hormones, and then you didn't go back on."

"Pretty much," she said. "It wasn't the first time I'd gone off them, but I knew that if I actually got pregnant and brought a baby into the world, I was going to want to be that baby's *mother*, that I would want to breastfeed him and care for him and… like maybe it shouldn't make a difference, but I wasn't going to be anyone's *father*."

"Obviously, it does make a difference," he said quietly.

She felt like crying, thinking about all this. She downed the rest of her drink and began attacking her baked potato.

"I'm sorry," he said. "I should have changed the subject, after all."

"It's fine," she said.

"I don't have any kids," he said. "I'm too old now."

"You're not too old," she said, looking up at him. "You're what? Thirty-eight? Thirty-nine?"

"It's not happening," he said. "I'm horrible with women. I'm even worse with kids. I mean, I don't have a lot of experience. I have a stepdaughter, but she's…" He shrugged. "Besides, I'm kind of a mess. I'm really screwed up."

She had thought this same thing, only a half hour before. "Well… you know… we'll get him locked up again, and that'll… you'll…"

He bowed his head.

"Sorry," she whispered. "I'm screwed up too."

He raised his gaze to hers. "You're not. You're… strong and brave and determined and… and amazing."

She was blushing again.

# CHAPTER THIRTEEN

When they walked back to their hotel rooms, Dawson intended to go into hers, but Liam invited her in for a drink, and she discovered he'd brought two large bottles of bourbon along with him. Wow, he was planning on drinking all of that alone?

More bad signs. This man was like a flashing red stoplight.

She shouldn't even agree to the drink.

But she found herself sitting at the little desk in his room, sipping bourbon out of a cardboard cup and staring into his eyes. They seemed to keep finding themselves doing that.

They weren't even talking, just gazing at each other and bringing the cups to their lips. The liquor was working through her body, into her belly, and she felt warm and drunk and brave and good.

He reached out and ran his fingers over the stubble on her jaw line.

She gasped.

He pulled his fingers back. "Sorry."

"I'm going to get it lasered, maybe," she said. "I don't know. It's expensive."

"I wish you wouldn't," he breathed.

She melted, her expression turning to liquid. "You…"

He smiled at her, and she was starting to find that smile of his somewhat irresistible, despite everything.

She sat forward, moving closer to him.

He sat forward too.

Their faces came closer.

She knew she should stop this, but she didn't. She only moved closer.

And then... their lips met, and it was like cotton candy, full of pink sugar-spun whimsy.

He leaned in and slid his hand around to cup the back of her skull, his thumb rubbing against her earlobe.

She opened her mouth, and he tasted like bourbon, and his tongue was this eager thing that slid against hers. She grabbed a fistful of his shirt and tugged him closer.

This made him stumble out of his chair.

And so she got out of hers too.

Then they were standing together, and he had her in his arms. He had broad shoulders and big arms, and she fit against him, and they were touching everywhere, the length of him pressed into her, and his hand was on her back, on her waist.

The kiss went on for a long time.

When it was over, she extricated herself from him, went over to the table, and drank the rest of the bourbon in her cup. She had her back to him. "Okay, well, that was... that was good. Good kiss." She seized the bottle of bourbon and poured more into her cup. "I shouldn't be here," she said as she sat down.

"Probably not," he agreed. He sat down next to her and poured himself some more bourbon too.

"I think I skipped the risky part of my adolescence," she said. "Maybe I skipped the part where I was attracted to the wrong kind of man."

He set down the bourbon bottle. "Ouch," he said lightly.

"Sorry," she said, drinking another swallow of fiery liquor.

"No," he said. "You're right. I'd be bad for you."

"But you want me," she said. "I'm not sure I'm

particularly attractive to a large pool of people.”

“That’s completely—”

“It’s the truth!” She sipped the bourbon and then set it down. “I’m not saying it because of how I feel about myself. I just recognize that being... the way I am... most men don’t want a woman who’s...”

“I don’t think I’ve ever been as attracted to someone as I am to you.”

That went through her like a sharp gust of wind. She couldn’t breathe.

He looked away, embarrassed. “I’ve had too much to drink.”

She let out a little giggle. “That’s exactly what the wrong kind of man would say. Something like that.”

He nodded. “Yeah.” A beat. “Sorry.”

She took a deep breath. “I can’t kiss you.”

“No,” he agreed. He drank more. “You really can’t.”

“There are a zillion reasons,” she said.

“I know,” he said.

“Not least of which is the fact it’s unprofessional.” She rubbed her forehead. “If anyone found out, if Captain Moore found out, for instance? He’d pull me off this.”

“Oh.” Liam furrowed his brow. “I hadn’t thought of that.”

“I can’t get pulled off this.” She twisted her fingers together.

“We’ll just pretend it never happened,” he said. “It doesn’t offend me if you want that. I completely understand.”

She took another drink of bourbon. “I think that’s best.”

“Okay,” he said.

She got up, looking him over. “I’m really sorry.”

“No, don’t be sorry,” he said.

“I’m going to be so embarrassed in the morning. I never drink this much.”

"Don't be embarrassed," he said. "Blame it on me. It's my fault. Yeah?"

She gave him a small smile. "You might not be as much of the wrong sort of man as I think you are."

"No, I think I am," he said.

She didn't know how to leave. She gestured at the door. "I should, um…"

"Yeah, of course." He nodded.

Then they stared at the floor awkwardly for long, long moments before she actually lurched towards the door.

* * *

Liam woke in the dark to a series of beeps on his phone—notifications that he was getting texts or something. He swiped his phone sleepily off the bedside table, hoping it wasn't some app that had decided to send him a series of texts about sale prices at 3:00 in the morning.

It was Hernandez.

*New chapter is up.*

*Are you reading this?*

*Holy hell, when you get this, call me back, so we can analyze.*

*Are you awake?*

Liam didn't respond to the text. Instead, he pulled up the fanfiction site on the internet to see if he could read the chapter. He got three paragraphs in before he got another text from Hernandez.

*I know it's rude to text in the middle of the night, but we're trying to catch a serial killer here.*

Liam texted back to tell Hernandez he was reading the chapter.

He went back to it, reading as quickly as he could. The chapter seemed relatively short. Not much was happening. Cindy was recovering from having her limbs removed and then reattached, and she and Frank were having a conversation about why Joe was coming after

Frank after all this time.

Cindy said that it couldn't be about her, because she wasn't with Frank anymore, and Joe obviously didn't want her back if he was capturing her and dismembering her. So she posited the idea that Joe had a fascination with Frank that might go beyond a simple conflict.

Liam rolled his eyes at this, because it was such a blatant attempt to turn *Hitgam* into *Dusk* Maddox/Cade slashfic. "Finn, did you ever even watch *Hitgam*? You should have kept this in the *Dusk* universe," he muttered at the screen.

Then Cindy looked up at Frank and said, "You can't tell me you've never thought about Joe and jacked off."

Liam got out of bed, gripping the phone, and headed for the adjoining door to Dawson's room.

# CHAPTER FOURTEEN

Freshman year of college was tough enough without worrying about drug dependency. Liam was never sure if Finn had intended for him to get hooked on ecstasy again when he dosed him with it, but Liam was determined that wouldn't happen. He would not allow himself to get too deeply into the drug, and he somehow convinced himself that the best way to do this was to use it again, so that he would be sure that it had no effect on him.

And to be on the safe side, Destiny should be there, too.

She'd be a good buffer between him and Finn, even if she was always teasing them that they were into each other.

So, the three of them ended up rolling their faces off in Destiny's apartment. The pills they got might have been cut with something else, because Liam thought they were a little speedy and they made him anxious. They seemed to have this same effect on Destiny.

Right around the time they were all peaking, she got weird and went to hide in the closet in her bedroom. She shut the door and wouldn't come out.

Liam and Finn tried to open the door and coax her out, but she kept slamming it in their faces, so eventually they gave up and sat on the floor in her bedroom, talking to her through the door.

It was dark in the room, barely lit by lamps which had sheets thrown over them to mute their brightness. Too much brightness was painful on E. In the distance, some kind of house music was pulsing from the stereo in the living room of the apartment. Destiny's bed wasn't made and the covers slithered out onto the floor.

Finn sat with his back against the bed, tracing patterns on his knee.

Destiny kept asking them if they were making out yet.

"No," Liam kept saying, sullen.

"I'm not gay," Finn said. "Maybe Liam is, but I'm not."

"Pfft," said Destiny from inside the closet. "Liam is your sexual fantasy come to life, Finn."

"My sexual fantasy come to life isn't a person," said Finn.

"What? You're into bestiality?"

"No," said Finn. "I meant that it's not any one person. It could be anyone. It's about what I want to do to them."

"Ooh, this I want to hear," said Destiny. "What would you do? Tie them to the bedposts?"

"Maybe," said Finn. "But I think it would be hotter if I didn't have to physically restrain them, if I could command them just with a word. If they'd do whatever I told them to."

"And you'd make them what? Suck your cock and tickle your balls?" Destiny was giggling.

Liam was starting to feel uncomfortably aroused. "Let's stop talking about this."

"Mostly, *I'd* want to do things to *them*, I think," Finn said, musing over this, as if he hadn't truly thought it through. "I'd want them to be accepting and open and still."

Destiny snorted. "You want a living fuck doll, then?"

"Maybe," said Finn. "Something posable."

"You want to fuck a dead person," she said.

"No," said Finn. "That's disgusting."

"You know," said Destiny, "it's really only men that

can be necrophiliacs. Women can't have sex with a corpse if they can't make it achieve an erection."

Now, Liam was feeling disgusted. "Can we not talk about dead bodies?"

"Maybe rigor mortis makes it hard?" said Destiny. "What do you think? Is that something we could search on the internet, you think?"

"Stop it," Liam snapped.

"Oh," said Destiny. "Sorry, Liam, what's your sexual fantasy?"

"I want to change the subject entirely," said Liam.

"Because it's Finn, right?" said Destiny.

"It's not Finn." Liam was annoyed.

"Have you ever fantasized about Finn?" said Destiny.

Finn looked at Liam from across the room and grinned.

"No," said Liam, who was lying through his teeth about that.

"Oh, come on," said Destiny. "You can't tell me you've never thought about Finn and jacked off."

* * *

Dawson sat up straight in bed, disoriented. She didn't know where she was.

The room was dark. A door was opening.

There had been a banging noise before.

"Dawson," said a dark figure, coming through the door.

Her gun.

She had a gun, didn't she? It was in the safe below her bed, except she wasn't in her room, and this wasn't her bed, and —

"It's me, Dawson. I'm sorry. I should have kept knocking and waited for you to open the door, but I tried the knob, and it wasn't locked and —"

"Liam," she breathed. She took a mangled breath and reached over to turn on the light beside her bed. She was in a hotel room. Her gun was unloaded and in the suitcase across the room. The ammunition was in the drawer in her bedside table. She had considered locking it up, because there was a safe for valuables in the room, but it was extra, and she didn't know if the department would have sprung for the extra cost or not, and why was she thinking about this?

Liam was wearing a pair of plaid pajama pants and no shirt. Her gaze skittered over his bare skin. She didn't know where to look.

"Probable cause is a thing, right?" Liam was saying.

She yanked the covers on the bed up as a protective measure against his bare chest. He had a smattering of dark curls across his pecks. A few of them were gray. She found herself liking this for no reason she could discern. "A thing? Yes, it's a thing. Did you really wake me up to ask me that question? Is that even a question? I don't understand."

"I mean, I know we're waiting for a warrant on Destiny's old apartment, but if you have probable cause, you don't need a warrant. Is that right?"

"Technically," she said. "What happened?"

He thrust his phone at her.

She blinked at the brightness of the screen, which was filled with rows and rows of text.

He jammed his fingers at the screen. "That is something that Destiny said to me in a specific place in her apartment, and we need to go there, right freaking now, because there's something we need to find there. This is a message from Finn to me."

"I don't know if that's enough," she said.

"Well, who cares?" Liam snatched the phone back. "If we find him, and we arrest him, it won't matter if we found him in some place where we don't have a warrant. It's not like they're going to let him go. He escaped from prison."

She thought about this. She supposed he was right. She nodded. "Okay."

"Okay?"

"Okay," she said. "Let's go."

"Good," he said. He didn't move.

She didn't either. A few moments passed, and she found herself looking at his stomach, which wasn't entirely flat, but just had a slight, soft protrusion, which she also liked for some stupid reason.

Liam seemed to realize he was half-naked. "I'll... get dressed."

"Excellent idea," she said.

He turned on his heel and walked out of the room, pulling the adjoining door closed behind him.

She took a deep breath, shaking herself.

Belatedly, she realized that she was hungover from all the drinking she'd done the night before. She filled an empty bottle of water from the tap, splashed water on her face, and then surveyed herself in the mirror.

Her hair was in disarray. She wished he hadn't seen her like that. She touched the hair that was growing at her sideburns, which was all that seemed to be left of the full beard she used to have. It was amazing how it had gone away when she stopped testosterone. She wondered if these stray hairs would eventually stop growing too. She kept toying with the idea of waxing them, but that would mean she'd have to let them grow out at least a few centimeters, and she could never stand to wait that long.

Body hair removal was not one of her favorite things about being a woman.

She ducked her head under the sink, dried it with a towel, and then combed it quickly. She shrugged into the clothes she'd been wearing the night before—the jeans and sweater. If they were going to break in without a warrant, why not?

Liam was waiting outside her room when she

emerged, bouncing on the balls of his feet.

She had drunk the entire water bottle and filled it again. She felt like hell. She looked him over. "You think Slater's in that apartment?"

"It makes sense." Liam started to walk down the hallway toward the elevator.

She kept pace with him. "Does it?"

"It's a great place to hide out," said Liam.

"It's an obvious place to hide out," she said.

"Yeah, but he's playing games with me," said Liam. "He wants me to go there, or he wouldn't have posted that chapter."

"Which is why I doubt he's there," she said.

"Unless he wants to see me."

She touched her gun, which was inside her coat. If she had a chance this time, she couldn't hesitate with Slater. She'd have to shoot him, even if she'd rather bring him in alive. He should stand trial for his crimes.

She knew that there was no real "safe" place to shoot someone. There were arteries everywhere. A person could bleed out if a major one got hit. If she shot Slater, there was a chance he died, end of story.

She was so caught up in thinking about that, it took her until they were on the elevator to register the eagerness in Liam's voice. He *wanted* to see Slater.

*You kissed him*, she thought.

She was an idiot. She stared forward as the elevator descended to the bottom floor and tried to tell herself that it wouldn't matter, because she had told him that they couldn't kiss ever again, and that she wouldn't be so stupid as to invite anything romantic between them again.

Ugh, this was a nightmare.

But at least he wasn't acting weird about it this morning.

*No, he's just too excited about the prospect of seeing his serial killer lover to care about having kissed you. So, that's very comforting.* She grimaced.

When the elevator door opened, Liam was out of it like a shot.

She had to hurry to keep up with him. They got to her car and he waited impatiently for her to unlock the doors. Inside, he tapped his fingers on the dashboard as she buckled her seatbelt and got out the keys.

They pulled out of the parking lot and were finally on the road.

He sat forward, straining against the shoulder strap of his seatbelt, looking all around, as if he expected something to materialize out of the darkness.

It made her feel on edge. It was colder here in Delaware than it had been in Virginia. Only a few degrees, but she felt it. In the early morning, before the sun had risen, it was a frosty, shadowed, empty world. No one else was on the road.

She had to struggle not to drive far too fast, to go careening through the darkened streets and swerving round the corners. She went the speed limit, and Liam grew more and more agitated next to her.

Eventually, they arrived at the apartment, and they parked.

Liam was out of the car and up on the porch before she had even closed her car door.

He tried the door knob. Finding it locked, he turned back to her. "This way."

"What way?" she said.

He was already walking around the house, taking an overgrown stone walkway towards the back of the building.

The apartment was contained in a house that had been divided into apartments. Judging from the mailboxes out front, there were four units here. Destiny Worth's had been on the bottom floor.

There was a fence, but Liam reached over and unlocked the gate, and they were inside a small courtyard, also overgrown, as if no one had been back here in years.

Liam crossed to a back door. He tried that knob, which was also locked, but he pushed his shoulder into the door and rattled the doorknob purposefully, and the door sprang open. She supposed he had experience with the house, but she was surprised no one had fixed that in however long it had been—nearly twenty years?

The house was dark.

They entered a small, cavernous kitchen which had obviously been added to the house sometime after it had been built. It was an old building, probably several hundred years old. The kitchen was small but modern, but everything was covered in a layer of dust. The refrigerator stood open—defrosted, unplugged.

No one was using this apartment.

Liam swerved into an empty room with wooden floors that might have been a living room. He hurried through that room and down a short hallway. There were several doors opening onto various rooms, most of which were also empty. One looked like a bathroom.

Liam pushed open the door at the end of the hall, and he went directly across the room to a closet.

When he opened it, the scent of death hit Dawson's nostrils.

There was a body in there.

Liam saw it, uttered a cry, and practically cartwheeled backward, flailing his arms and legs in a mad attempt to get away from it.

Dawson pressed forward slowly, grimly determined to look. She took out her phone and turned on the flashlight app.

The body was male, and he was naked. He was lying on his back. There was a strip of paper taped to his stomach, just below his belly button, and Dawson knelt down to lower the flashlight so that she could read it.

It said, *Nothing ever eased that desperate ache.*

# CHAPTER FIFTEEN

Dawson thought it must be another line from a fanfic.

But no one could be sure. Liam thought it probably came from *This Love*, which was the fanfic that Slater had cut up and taped to his original victims. Liam wasn't familiar enough with it to know for certain.

She asked him if it meant anything particular to him, and he said it didn't.

Of course, that wasn't the first thing they talked about.

First, they left the apartment entirely and called in the local police, so that the scene could be processed. That was a lengthy affair, one that took hours at the scene, and then hours waiting at the station later. Then there were interviews, official statements to be given to the detectives who were handling the case.

So, it wasn't until nearly noon that she and Liam had a chance to really talk about anything.

The body was Kaveney, of course. He'd been killed in the same manner that all of Slater's victims were usually killed, a knife to the back of the skull. It was too soon to know if the body had been molested post-mortem.

Dawson's concern wasn't the body, but the apartment. She wanted to know who owned that place, and who was renting it out. It obviously hadn't been lived in for a very long time, and that was odd to her.

She got the name of the landlord easily enough. It was a matter of public record, and she found it on the county's website.

So, after she and Liam left the station, she suggested they get something to eat and then go pay the landlord a visit to find out what they could.

Liam was agreeable to this, and they were knocking on the landlord's door only a short time later.

The man who opened the door looked them both over warily.

Dawson wished she'd worn her suit and not jeans for only the twentieth time that day. She was also still nursing a hangover, although she felt better now that she had something in her stomach. She'd eaten a few donuts at the police station, but that hadn't done much except elevate her blood sugar and make her crash.

She showed the man her badge. "Mr. Graysmith? I'm Detective Haysle Dawson, and this is Liam Emerson. We're wondering if we could ask you a few questions."

"Is this about the body they found in one of my apartments?" said Graysmith. "Because I've already talked to the police today about that."

"We're curious who you rent that place to," she said.

"Don't you people talk to each other? I went over this." Graysmith glared at them.

"Sorry, just humor me and go through it once more?"

Graysmith sighed heavily. "All right, look. About ten years back, someone got in touch with me about the place, since they heard it was empty. They were willing to pay first month, security, last month, and a bonus to secure the place—but only if I waved the typical background check that I'd do for anyone moving in. I resisted, and they offered to pay me a full years' rent up front in addition to all that. I figured they might be doing something illegal, but I thought it was drugs or something, right? This is a college town. I just told them that I'd be by to inspect and if it was a meth lab, end of deal, right?" He shrugged.

"I assume you discovered nothing was there."

"Exactly," said Graysmith. "Someone wanted to pay me money to *not* live there. Well, that makes them the best tenant I've ever had, to be honest. No wear and tear on the place. No costly repairs. I go in once every couple of months and make sure there's no water damage starting or that there's not an infestation of mice, that kind of thing. Mostly, however, I've been pretty happy with the arrangement."

"They pay you every month?" said Dawson.

"Once a year," said Graysmith. "They pay all twelve months up front."

"With a check?" said Dawson.

"A PayPal account," said Graysmith. "I don't know anything about who it is, but every January, I get a chunk of change deposited in my account. All I have is an email address."

"Which is?" said Dawson.

"Maddoxlovescade@kmail.com," said Graysmith.

* * *

"Cute," Dawson was saying from the driver's side of the car as they drove away from speaking with the landlord.

Liam rested his forehead against the window, feeling thin and compressed, like he'd just come through a trash compactor. He should have known that they wouldn't actually find Finn in Destiny's apartment. That was too easy, like Dawson had said. Maybe it had been wishful thinking on his part.

Where the hell was Finn hiding?

"So, it's obviously been Slater renting that apartment," said Dawson. "Do we even need to prove that? Doesn't he sell fanart for *Dusk* online?"

"Did," said Liam. "Obviously, he can't anymore."

"Is his online store still up?"

"I don't know. What does it matter?"

"Maybe it's the same PayPal account," she said.

Liam dutifully got out his phone and began to navigate to the website where Finn had hawked his wares. "All his buy buttons are gone. There's a message his PayPal's been shut down to repeated reports of abuse." He set down the phone. "I bet people tried to buy things after the news broke that he was a serial killer, and there was no one to ship the merchandise to them. I'm kind of surprised Finn isn't paying someone to do that for him. He's going to need the income."

"Well, maybe he had a plan to do it himself after he escaped prison," said Dawson.

"Or maybe, now that he's pretty high profile, the copyright owners would decide to go after him in court. I imagine it's not great for the brand to be associated with dead sex workers."

"All good points," sighed Dawson. "I guess it doesn't matter. It only proves that he's been planning this for a long time or something? Why rent that place?"

"I wonder if he was going to take me there," Liam muttered. "I got the impression that having me in that cage was only the first part of his plan. But then, I also thought he was going to send me to jail for the murders once he'd created an airtight plan. Anyway, it doesn't matter. The important thing is that we have to find the bunker."

"The one that's underneath a parking lot?" said Dawson.

"He's found a way into it," said Liam. "That's where he is. I know it."

"How?"

"I don't know," he said. "But let's go to the parking lot and look around, see what we can find."

She considered. "Okay. But I want a shower first."

He turned to her, eyebrows raised. "Really?"

"Really," she said. "I'll escort you on your wild goose chase, Liam, but I'm sick of smelling the dead booze from last night seeping out of my pores." She blushed. "Sorry I said that. Thank you for not saying anything about last night."

"We're pretending that never happened." He lowered his voice conspiratorially.

She blushed deeper. "Right. Of course." She squared her shoulders.

"Fine," he said briskly, changing the subject. "Shower first. But it's not a wild goose chase."

* * *

When Liam finished his shower, he had the creepy feeling that someone else was in his hotel room.

He stood inside the shower, the curtain closed, water dripping off his body, and he softly called out Finn's name.

Of course, there was no answer.

He shook himself. This was stupid. How would Finn get into his hotel room? It wasn't as if Liam had left the key lying around.

He scoffed, and then he pulled the shower curtain aside.

From out in his room, he heard a noise, like a door creaking slowly closed.

A cold hand closed around his spine. He was all alone here, wet and naked, and he felt very vulnerable and very small. He'd never gotten into a physical altercation with Finn. Even when Finn had captured him, he'd come up on him from behind and used the taser to incapacitate him.

He instinctively knew, however, that he'd be no match against Finn.

Finn would subdue him, easily, efficiently, and then press into him, their bodies close—something that made Liam feel horrified and also electrified—and he'd have complete and utter control.

Liam convulsed. He stood there, dripping on the floor,

waiting for Finn to come through the door.

Moments passed, one after another, and the door didn't open.

Maybe he hadn't heard anything. Maybe it had been his mind playing tricks on him. He picked up a towel and wrapped it around his waist. Like most hotel towels, it was too small to really cover much, and it gapped when he walked, exposing most of his upper thighs.

But he walked with a purpose anyway, forcefully out of the bathroom, gritting his teeth against his shameful fear.

The hotel room was exactly how he'd left it before he'd gotten in the shower. His suitcase was open on the bed, where he'd left it when he'd gotten his shampoo and soap out of it.

And the door was open.

Not a lot, but a little bit. He obviously hadn't closed it when he'd come in and the noise he'd heard had been his door creaking wider open.

He shot across the room and slammed it shut, sucking in a shaky breath.

He turned back to his room, the steam from the shower floating out into the room, making the top of the mirrors out here foggy.

Another thought occurred to him. Maybe Finn had come in through that door and left it open to indicate that he was there.

*Finn is not in my room,* he assured himself.

He went and looked under the bed, and there was nothing there, but his towel fell off.

He snatched it back up, horrified at the idea of Finn seeing him naked, as if that hadn't already happened before. His hands shook as he tucked the towel closed.

*Better check the closet,* he said to himself.

He sucked in a steadying breath and started toward the closet door. He would open it up, and nothing would be in there, and then he'd be fine, and he could stop—

His phone started to ring.

Liam halted. He eyed the closet door. He couldn't bear to put his back to it, so he backed up until he could pick up his phone from the bed.

Keeping one eye on the closet door, he answered it. "Hello?"

"It's me, Ricky Hernandez. You never texted me back, and now I hear there's another body?"

"Oh," he said. "Sorry about that."

"You have to keep me in the loop here if you want my help."

"Well," said Liam, still staring at the closet door, "your expertise is in fanfiction, right? This was about me. It was about something that happened when I was with Finn." He put the phone on speaker and set it on the bed. "Can you still hear me?"

"I can hear you fine," said Hernandez. "But I just want to point out that you weren't even looking for a new chapter, and if I hadn't told you that one was posted—"

"I was looking. I just got... distracted," said Liam, yanking on some clothes as quickly as he could. This way, when he opened the closet door, he'd be dressed, and that would be better than grappling naked with Finn. So much better.

"What distracted you?"

*Haysle Dawson*, he thought. "Sleeping."

"Oh, funny," said Hernandez. "Well, listen, I don't need to sleep. I'll monitor this fanfic day and night, and you need me. So keep me in the damned loop."

Hmm... Dawson. Maybe he should get *her* to open the closet door. She had a gun.

"I'm sorry," said Liam. "Really. Look, if another chapter gets posted, call me right away, day or night, all right?"

"Of course I will," said Hernandez.

"Great," said Liam. "Dawson and I are going out to do some investigation, so if that's the only reason you called…?"

"I don't mean to be a dick about it," said Hernandez. "It's just that it's frustrating to hear things second hand."

"I'll make sure to update you from now on."

"I would appreciate that."

A knock on his hotel room door.

Liam started. He looked from the closet door to the hotel room door. "Uh, I have to hang up now."

"Okay," said Hernandez.

"Okay," said Liam. "Bye." He hung up the phone and walked across the room without ever putting his back to the closet door, feeling more and more ridiculous as he did so.

When he opened the door, Dawson was standing there.

She raised her eyebrows. "You ready?"

"Uh…" He glanced at the closet door. Now that she was standing here, he couldn't ask her to look. It was ridiculous, and it made him sound like a little boy, afraid of the boogeyman. "Yeah, I'm ready." His coat was hanging on a rack by the door. He checked his pocket for his room key, which was there, and then he shoved his phone in next to it.

He stepped out of the room and shut the door behind him.

# CHAPTER SIXTEEN

Liam surveyed the parking lot, which stretched out in front of him, empty except for a few stray cars. The parking had once been a field behind the practice football field, and it had once contained the entrance to the bunker.

It was later in the day, and the campus tended to clear out after all the commuting students drove home. This parking lot was pretty far away from the main part of campus, anyway, so it wouldn't be used unless everything else was full.

"So," said Dawson, next to him, "this bunker, did you go there often?"

"Yeah, a lot our senior year," said Liam said. "Destiny's the one who found it. We never did find out who it belonged to. It was like a relic from another time. It must have been made in the Cold War era or something. It was stocked with all these shelves of canned goods and there was a room with bunks on the walls. We went there, and we kept expecting someone to find out we were using it, but no one ever did. And now they've covered it up with a parking lot."

"About where was the entrance?" said Dawson.

Liam didn't know. He stared out at the pavement, and he couldn't even remember what this field had looked like before. Everything was different.

"Maybe that doesn't matter," said Dawson. "You think he's got some alternate way in? If he constructed his own bunker out at that cabin, maybe he found a way to tunnel into this one."

"Right." Liam turned to look at her. "We'll go walk around the perimeter of the parking lot, looking for disturbed ground or something."

"Great," she said.

He sighed. "You think I'm insane."

"I don't think that about you at all." She gave him a smile, and he realized that he was liking the way she smiled far too much. "But I'm not sure we're going to find this bunker."

Maybe he didn't even want to find it. Maybe if he went in there, he'd be forced to face what had happened in there or… or worse.

Maybe she was still in there.

A wave of revulsion went through him at that.

It was possible. He'd never gone back to the bunker after that night.

"What exactly happened in this bunker?" Dawson was starting to walk about the perimeter of the parking lot.

He kept pace with her, casting his glance here and there along the ground. "It was just a place we partied."

"Slater said something to you about 'that night,'" said Dawson.

He licked his lips.

"I don't mean to push at things that are uncomfortable," said Dawson, "and I know you didn't want to talk about it before, but I think we need to talk about it. You say that you left Slater and Destiny… in an intimate situation, and then you never saw her again."

"Yes."

"What else can you tell me?"

This was what he'd told her, that the night had been about Finn wanting to have sex with Destiny, but… well, it wasn't exactly a lie, but it did leave things out. Still, it was as good a thing to explain as any, and there was no way he could ever talk about what had happened using words. When he thought about it, he couldn't verbalize anything about it, even in his head. It was just a series of images and sensations and a wide pit of awful that yawned open inside him. He cleared his throat. "Finn wanted to share things with me," he said. "He wanted to share her, and I let him, and then I... I don't know, I didn't want to watch them together, so I remember leaving, and then I don't remember anything else."

The blacking out wasn't a lie. He *had* blacked out after all of it. Why he couldn't mercifully have blacked it *all* out he didn't know.

"You don't remember because you were drinking?"

"That's right."

"Was she...?" She licked her lips. "And Destiny was... she consented to this?"

He couldn't speak. Did she *know?*

"Liam? Was she unconscious when you left?"

He forced himself to speak. "It wasn't like that. He wasn't raping her." The words came out more smoothly than he expected them to.

Dawson stopped walking.

He kept going.

Her voice carried from behind him. "If he was, and you didn't say anything, just like you didn't say anything before, and you don't want to admit that—"

"No, she liked the idea of it. I think she always had a thing for him," he said. "I think she was eager enough for it all." That was true. She hadn't been stupid, that was the thing. And she hadn't been a saint. She'd been flawed and interesting and sexy, and she hadn't deserved what had happened to her in that bunker.

So help him, if he found her body...

Dawson caught up to him. "Listen, you can trust me. I know you feel guilty about a lot of things, but you don't need to. You were a victim, Liam. He victimized you. He's still doing it."

Liam glanced at her. "Yeah, I know."

Maybe it would be better to find her body. Maybe that was exactly what he needed. Maybe the lies were the worst of it. Carrying this around with him for all this time… maybe that was what he couldn't bear anymore.

Dawson was studying him, her expression concerned.

No.

No, he didn't want her to know the truth of it.

He picked up the pace, and she matched him.

They walked around the parking lot once and then walked around again and again in ever-widening circles so that they could look to see if the ground had been disturbed or if they could see anything at all that might indicate Finn had accessed the tunnel.

Eventually, they were exhausted, and they'd found nothing.

Dawson got a text from someone at the CCPD asking her to call them back. She said her phone was low on battery, and that they should go back to the hotel so that she could charge it and call them back. Afterward, she said they could have dinner together and she'd tell him what was going on. They could also talk about what their next move might be if they wanted to find Finn.

He was paranoid that her phone had plenty of battery and that she just didn't want him to overhear her conversation with the police department.

He was probably paranoid only because of being forced to confront himself out here. He was untrustworthy. He was a liar.

They drove back to the hotel in silence.

They took the elevator up to their floor and walked down the hallway to their rooms. He took out his key card and opened the door. She opened hers as well.

"I'll knock on the adjoining door when I'm ready, all

right?"

"Sure," he said, wondering if he'd be able to listen to her phone call through the walls.

He shut the door behind him and looked up.

His bed wasn't the way he'd left it.

The covers were turned down, and there was something on his pillow.

He stifled a cry.

He knew what was there, and he'd better be quiet. He didn't want Dawson to come and investigate. He crossed the bed and snatched up what lay there.

It was a tiny scrap of filmy fabric, a pair of underwear that had belonged to Destiny. Back then, the style was for girls to wear thong underwear and very low-rise jeans so that the back of the underwear would be visible whenever they sat down or bent over or shook their butts on the dance floor in clubs.

He couldn't count the number of times he'd been sitting in class behind some girl whose thong was on display and how fucking distracting that had been when he was nineteen years old and a flaming ball of hormones.

Liam's hands shook as his fingers tightened around the lingerie.

He turned slowly, to look at the closet door.

He'd left it closed, he remembered, because he'd wanted Dawson to come and open it for him.

The closet door was open now. Inside there was a fold-out ironing board attached the wall and a set of hangers that couldn't be removed from the closet rod.

Finn wasn't in there. Not anymore.

Liam hurried to the bathroom, thrusting open the door and turning on the light. When the light came on, so did a noisy fan.

The bathroom was empty.

He pushed the shower curtain aside.

Nothing in there but a small cluster of his own hair

around the drain. He thought of the maid who'd have to clean that, took pity on her, fished it out, and put it in the trash.

He looked under the bed again.

Finn was gone.

Liam sat down on the bed and brought both of his fists to his forehead, including the one that still held Destiny's thong.

What game was Finn playing?

What did he want?

* * *

"They're still waiting on DNA for the limbs that we found in the bouquet," Dawson was saying. They were back in the steakhouse connected to the hotel, and Liam was trying to focus on whatever she was saying, but it was hard, because he'd taken a Tylenol with codeine and washed that down with several pulls from the bourbon bottle. He'd also ordered a drink to have with dinner, but he'd downed that too quickly. He felt blurred out, as if the sharp edges of the world were gone, and that was how he wanted to feel, but he remembered now that he had been paranoid and that he'd been curious about this phone call Dawson had received.

He blinked at her. "They called you to tell you that they don't have results?"

"No," she said. "They called to tell me that they identified the Jane Doe who shot herself."

"Oh," he said. They were sitting in a booth. He leaned against the back of it and surveyed Dawson, trying to look interested, trying to keep his eyes open. He *was* interested, but he was also high and more than a little drunk.

"Her name is Annie Gibbons," said Dawson. "She went missing five years ago, from — get this — one of those MadCad conventions." This was what the people who were fans of Maddox/Cade slash called themselves.

169

MadCads. "A convention where Slater was selling his fanart."

"Huh." Liam was having trouble processing this.

"He must have captured her," said Dawson. "Years ago, and kept her somewhere, like he did with you. I think he… brainwashed her. That stuff she was saying to us about sacrifice and love and that sort of thing? I mean, I think he planted a suggestion in her brain, and she shot herself because Slater made her do it."

Liam rubbed his chin. "You think he brainwashed her?"

"What? You don't think he's capable of that?" Dawson spread her hands. "I saw the way you are with him. He did something to you."

Liam shook his head. "No. It's not like that."

"What's it like?"

"He's… there's something about him. When I'm around him, I feel…"

"Yes, he's got charisma," said Dawson. "I felt that. I imagine that when he turns the charm on, he's hard to resist."

"I'm not brainwashed." He was offended. Well, he wasn't actually offended, because right now, he felt nothing but fuzz. But he felt as though if he were actually feeling anything, he would feel offended, so he was trying to approximate a reaction that resembled offense.

"Okay," she said. She was patronizing him.

"I would never shoot myself," he said.

"No," she said. "But maybe you would have if you'd been in that dog crate for five years."

He considered this. It was a sobering thought. He was fairly sure that living in those conditions for that long would have driven him insane.

Dawson wasn't paying attention to him now. "It's only… the scope of this… it's getting bigger and bigger now. Where was he keeping her? It must have been somewhat close if he was keeping her alive, right? But he had you in that bunker, and there was no one else with you, so she must have been in another location. How did he manage all that and to keep up with his job and to have an active social life, which everyone attests that he did?"

"I don't know," said Liam. Something about this seemed wrong, though. Finn might keep him in a cage, yes, but not some random girl he captured at a convention. He wouldn't do that, anyway.

*Jealous, tiger?*

He stiffened. "Finn killed sex workers. He didn't capture women from conventions."

"We don't know what he did," said Dawson. "There may be a lot of things that he was doing that we have no idea about."

"This isn't…" He shook his head. "This isn't *Finn.* That's not what he would do."

"Why not?" said Dawson.

"He's… simpler," said Liam. "It's an impulse for him. This elaborate planning, it doesn't *fit.*"

"You don't think capturing you and trying to frame you for his own murders wasn't an elaborate plan?"

He furrowed his brow. She was right. He wished his brain was functioning, so that he could think this through, or so he could even find the right words to talk about it.

"Listen," said Dawson quietly, "you witnessed his early incarnation, in which he was drugging girls and raping them. But by your own admission, he didn't start killing until Destiny, right? So, the deaths of the other girls in college, the ones who you say went missing? You can't be sure what he did with them. Maybe he kept them prisoner."

"He didn't do that with his current victims," said Liam. "The sex workers. He picked them up, watched them eat, killed them, and then he raped them and dumped them."

"True," said Dawson, and now she was furrowing her brow. "I'm no expert on serial killers, but that does seem odd for him to vary his tactic."

"Exactly," said Liam.

"But maybe he's just that intelligent and that creative," said Dawson.

Liam didn't say anything.

"Listen," said Dawson, "even when he was only a rapist, that took planning and deliberation. He had to find some way to drug them, and he had to get it into their drinks unsuspecting."

"It's a lot different than keeping someone captive for five years and brainwashing them to kill themselves," said Liam. "What does Finn get out of it, anyway?"

"The ultimate power over a person," said Dawson. "He gets her to take her own life."

"But it's about the rape," said Liam. He was certain of this.

"But it's like we were talking about. Rape is about power, too," said Dawson.

Liam didn't say anything.

The waiter brought their food then.

"Maybe we shouldn't talk about this while we're eating," said Dawson.

"Sure," said Liam. It wasn't easy for him to talk, anyway.

# CHAPTER SEVENTEEN

Back in his hotel room, Liam drank more bourbon and passed out face down on top of the covers. He didn't dream. He was just in a pool of empty blackness for some unspecified time and then he woke up suddenly.

There was no noise in the room, nothing like that, but out of nowhere, he was alert.

He rolled over onto his back. His head was pulsing painfully. It felt as if someone had stabbed him directly through his temples. Usually the codeine would dim that. Why wasn't the codeine working? Hadn't he taken enough?

Oh, he'd taken the pill early, and then he hadn't taken more before bed, not like he usually would.

His closet door was still open. He couldn't bear to close it. He'd also unlocked the adjoining door to Dawson's room in case he needed her and her gun. He couldn't stop looking into the closet. It was a shadowed, sinister cave. He had the urge to go in there and close himself inside, to curl up in a ball and hide away.

*It'll be like being back in the crate,* he thought.

He shuddered, peeling back the covers and crawling under them.

As he did, his hands brushed the cool smoothness of his phone.

Ah, the phone with its portal to social media and the internet and pictures of cats. Comfort and safety and civilization.

He burrowed under the covers and began scrolling through various things on his phone. The light from the screen made his head hurt worse, but he didn't care. He wasn't getting out of this bed. He couldn't stand the idea of leaving it. Irrationally, he felt safe here.

He found himself checking the fanfiction site.

There was a new chapter.

His finger hovered over the link. He didn't want to read it. Reading it was letting Finn in, and Finn was already too far in.

*All the way in, tiger.*

He slammed the phone down against the bed. His breath came in noisy gasps.

Slowly, he found himself picking up the phone again.

*No*, he begged himself. *Nononono.*

He clicked the link. He began to read. That yawning awful feeling opened up inside him. He had almost missed it.

* * *

"I want to unread it." Hernandez's voice was shaking. "I want to claw my eyes out."

Liam was propped up in the bed, cradling the phone against his ear with his shoulder. He was drinking a glass of water. He felt calm. "It wasn't so bad."

"It's like…" Hernandez trailed off. "It seduces you. It starts off playful and a little soft, and it's… it's sexy."

Liam swallowed.

"And then it turns on you," said Hernandez. "Then it shows its true horridness and you're sitting there with this awful sea of revulsion surging inside you, but you're still half-aroused. It uses your body against you."

"Let's stop talking about it," Liam decided.

"I called you to talk about it," said Hernandez.

"Right," said Liam. "Okay, well, but that's so we can try to figure out what it means, so let's talk about it from that angle instead."

"Sure," said Hernandez.

Silence.

"It doesn't evoke any memories within me," said Liam. "This isn't like anything that ever happened to me."

"Maybe it didn't make *you* aroused," said Hernandez. "Maybe I shouldn't have said that. Maybe I shouldn't have shared. I don't know if that was really unprofessional or something. I didn't mean—maybe there's just something wrong with me—"

"There's nothing wrong with you," said Liam. He sighed, taking pity on the other man. "It's… I think that's how anyone would react. It made me feel…" But then he couldn't finish the sentence.

"I'm sorry," said Hernandez. "I'm really sorry. I'm doing this wrong. It's only that I'm starting to feel out of my depth here. If this was on one of the more mainstream fanfiction sites, it might be taken down, because it's that bad. But this site… this is kind of the wild west of fanfiction. Anything goes. And I've read some strange, strange things in my time, but this is different."

"I think it's like *This Love*," said Liam. "*This Love* was a fantasy of something he wanted to happen between me and him."

"What? He wanted you to kill a girl together and then screw each other next to her dead body?"

"That never happened."

"Of course it didn't!" Hernandez was horrified at the mere suggestion.

Liam stretched his neck, putting his hand up to hold the phone in place. "He wants to do this to me. He's going to get to me and take me someplace and tie me to a chair and then we're going to have a meal together. The rest of it… the other parts… well, I won't cooperate with that."

"He's not going to take you," said Hernandez. "You need to go and wake up Dawson."

"I'm not sure what I think about the choice of venue," Liam mused. "In *Hitgam*, the characters all live in that house. It's sort of analogous to a fraternity house, only they don't call it a fraternity on the show, they call it a guild, and guilds can have both male and female members. So, I'd think it would be the dorm. It would be Renwick. But Renwick is abandoned, and it's practically falling down, so I don't see how he's going to do it there."

"You're taking this pretty well, considering it's a personal threat," said Hernandez.

"Finn doesn't see it as a threat. It's like sexting to him."

"I still think you should be more worried."

Liam didn't answer. The desire to see Finn, it was still there, just like it had been when Dawson had come to his door and proposed visiting Finn in jail. He wanted to go and find Finn.

Maybe he *was* brainwashed.

He chuckled a little. That would make it all so easy, wouldn't it? Then he'd be completely exonerated of all blame and wrongdoing. Finn *made* him do it.

"Are you laughing?" said Hernandez, incredulous. "What's funny about this?"

"Nothing." His voice was flat.

"Look, he says something about how they're Eskimo brothers, how they've both screwed Cindy?"

"Sure," said Liam. "He says that happened in Ash House, which it did on *Hitgam*." It was the bunker. Finn was in the bunker. But Liam couldn't find the damned bunker.

"Well, but you said nothing like that ever happened with you and Finn, so I don't know why I brought that up," said Hernandez. "It's only… that Destiny person you talk about? Didn't you think that she was Cindy?"

"But it wasn't her arms and legs in the bouquet," said Liam. "So, I don't know anything." He sighed. "Look, it's the middle of the night. How about we both sleep on this, and I'll call you in the morning."

"You can go back to sleep?" said Hernandez. "I guess you're more desensitized to this."

"I guess," said Liam. What he thought was, *It's worse to imagine it. When it really happens, it's just real, and there's nothing there except the physicality of it.*

He and Hernandez hung up.

Liam took off his pajamas and got dressed. He took a look at himself in the mirror. He ran a hand through his hair ruefully, and then a wet comb.

He shrugged into his coat and opened the door to his hotel room. Striding down the hallway, he stared at the elevator looming in front of him. He took the elevator to the bottom floor and then went out the front door.

He was on the opposite side of town from campus, but this little college town was small, and he could make the trip in about twenty minutes, if he walked briskly. It was cold, and he would want to walk briskly.

He hunched his shoulders and stuck his hands in his pockets and took off into the darkness.

# CHAPTER EIGHTEEN

The first time they found the bunker, they were out behind the practice field taking ecstasy. They were older then, and it had been years since they'd taken it together as freshmen. They had come out here so that they could look at the night sky, at the stars overhead.

It was late fall, and they all lay on their backs with their heads together, their feet pointing outward like the points of a star.

Destiny was talking about death, and about rebirth, and about how the stars were made from the same elements that made up everything on earth, and how everything was connected, and how death wasn't really death.

Liam thought that was beautiful, but then he was on E, and everything was beautiful.

He and Destiny had been off-again for most of junior year and first quarter of senior year. She had been busily working on some art project that she kept secret from everyone, and she'd been skipping all her classes. Even now, she wasn't technically a senior like Finn and Liam. She didn't have enough credits.

Sometimes, Finn would claim to have seen Destiny during this off-again period, and he always made it seem like something had been going on with the two of them, which hadn't bothered Liam at the time, because he had been happy not to be in a relationship with Destiny.

Destiny was exhausting, and she was strange, and

junior year had been easier without her in it. He had vowed, up and down, inside and outside, that he and Destiny were *never getting back together* again.

And yet, here he was, back with Destiny, who had gotten stranger and more intriguing in the time they'd been apart. Now, she liked to play kinky games with him whenever they went to bed together. Hot wax and clamps and breath play, the latter of which made Liam incredibly uncomfortable but in a bothersome way that also turned him on.

He liked it better when she did it to him, but he felt he had to reciprocate, so he would wrap his hands around her neck and squeeze and she would lock eyes with him, daring him to push it further and further and further…

Once, she passed out.

It only lasted a few seconds, actually, but they were the longest seconds of his life.

He had crawled off of her panicking, gaping at her, thinking in terror of the 911 call he was going to have to make and how was he going to explain this, and should he get her dressed, and—

She woke up.

She was annoyed the sex had stopped, but he'd been too freaked out by the entire thing to perform. That had effectively ended that session, and he was always more careful with her after that, never going so far, even though she would sometimes ask him to do it again, would show him the places on her neck where he should push.

Even with all that, even though he somehow dreaded it, he found himself returning to the idea of it whenever he masturbated. This disturbed him, and he tried to actively dissuade it—thinking of other things, watching porn online (which was not necessarily an easy thing to do when one shared a room with another person), whatever he could think of, and always—if he wanted to climax—he had to return to imagining it, to imagining his hands on her neck.

He wouldn't have been thinking about it when he was on the field there, but Destiny started talking about near-death experiences, which lead easily to the idea of having a near-death experience while having sex, and then some speculation on the idea of the little death, and some scene in *Antony and Cleopatra* which was all about dying and having an orgasm at the same time and how Destiny thought this was cool, not creepy.

Liam thought it was strange that Destiny had actually read any Shakespeare or that she'd shown up to a class long enough to hear it discussed.

And Finn had gotten up and begun crawling around the field, running his fingers over the blades of grass, ignoring both of them.

That was how they found the bunker. Finn fell into it. The opening was covered over with a square of grass and sod, and over time, this had grown together, but when Finn put too much weight on the door to it, it gave way. The door had been designed to open upward, but it was old, and the wood had rotted and broken.

Later, they would make a new door for it so that there wasn't a big, obvious hole in the middle of the field.

They'd descended down the ladder into the place, and it had been too nifty for words. It was before *Lost* aired on TV, but when Liam had seen that episode, he'd gotten chills and then he'd had to run to the bathroom to throw up. He'd lost interest in the show after that.

This bunker didn't have electricity or cool 1950s era furniture. It was mostly a hole in the ground, but it was *their* hole in the ground, and they felt special for having discovered it. Maybe the fact that they'd all been rolling their faces off when they found it had been part of it too.

He remembered that they had pulled one of the mattresses off the bunks that hung from chains on the wall and set it on the concrete floor. They'd all sat together, Destiny in the middle, and they'd decided that the ecstasy gods, whoever they might be, had gifted this place to them, and that it belonged to the three of them.

"We can't tell anyone about it," said Destiny. "It's just for the three of us."

Both he and Finn agreed to this readily.

Then Finn made another rule. "No coming down here unless we're all three here. It's for the three of us, but *only* the three of us."

Destiny turned to him. "Poor Phineas, still feeling like the third wheel." She leaned over and kissed Finn, right in front of Liam, and Liam felt a burst of black envy and discomfort even through the haze of serotonin pumping out from his brain. Destiny immediately pulled away from Finn and kissed Liam. Liam was still too shocked by the sight of Finn and Destiny to even respond.

"Now," said Destiny tittered, "you two kiss."

Liam shook his head.

"Come on," said Destiny. "It's not like you never have."

Finn leaned around Destiny, smiling at Liam. "Don't be selfish, tiger. Your girl wants a show." He ran his thumb over Liam's bottom lip.

Liam's body sparked with the drug and the way he always responded to Finn. He leaned forward and pressed his lips into Finn's.

Destiny sucked in an audible breath, delighted.

* * *

Liam arrived at the parking lot and told himself he was seeing things, even though he knew he wasn't.

He had a moment of hesitation, where he thought about dialing Dawson, because maybe she should know, and he wondered what the hell it was that he was doing here at all.

But these thoughts didn't seem to work their way

through him, not all the way, and he was moving across the pavement even as he thought them, walking with a purpose toward the supine form in the middle there. When he reached the motionless body, he lay down with his head close to the form.

"Hey there, tiger," said Finn in a low, rich voice.

"Hi, Finn," he murmured.

"It's just us now," said Finn.

"Yeah," said Liam.

Finn rolled over onto his side, propping himself up on one elbow. "Did you miss me?"

"Of course." Liam stayed on his back, but he turned to face Finn.

Finn reached out with his other hand and used his forefinger to trace a line down Liam's cheek. "I missed you, too."

Liam shut his eyes. "I know what you want."

"Is that so?"

"I read the chapter you posted."

Finn's finger was running over Liam's jaw now. "That was just an invitation, tiger. I hoped you'd come."

"I'll..." Liam's voice was choked. "I'll eat with you—*for* you. You can even... you can do things. But..."

Finn's finger grazed Liam's throat. "I can do whatever I want with you, tiger. Say it."

"No," said Liam. He knocked Finn's hand away. "No. None of this makes sense, Finn. I want you to explain it to me. I want to understand about the girl in the warehouse and what freezer you've got full of body parts and how this all works. Why did you say that thing about killing being the pinnacle experience of existence? You know, that doesn't sound like something you would say. It sounds like something that..." Now, the bottom of his voice dropped out. "That *she* would say."

"She changed me," said Finn. "Didn't she change you, too?"

Liam turned away. His lower lip was trembling.

"I want you to let me put you in handcuffs," said Finn. "Yes?"

Liam looked back at him. "I said I'd eat with you. I came to you. Why does it have to be—"

"Because I can't trust you, tiger."

"I didn't tell the detective what I was doing. I didn't tell anyone. I think part of me is hoping you'll just kill me this time."

"Let me handcuff you, then."

Liam swallowed again. "Fine."

Finn sat up, crossing his legs and coming out with the handcuffs. They glittered in the moonlight, dangling from his hand. "Sit up."

Liam sat up.

"Hold out your hands," said Finn. "I'll let you have them in front. It'll be hard for you to eat otherwise."

Liam bit down on his bottom lip. His throat was scratchy.

Finn watched him expectantly.

Liam offered Finn his wrists. A tear spilled down his cheek. He didn't know why he was crying. Was it for himself, or only because he was afraid? He wished he hadn't come.

No.

That wasn't true. He wanted to wish that, but he didn't.

Going to Finn was right somehow. He felt it. He knew it.

Finn brushed the tear away and planted a kiss on Liam's cheekbone.

Liam made a strangled noise and jerked back.

But Finn had already closed one handcuff on his wrist, so Liam didn't get very far.

"Liam," Finn's voice was gentle but disapproving.

Liam gave him his other wrist.

Finn snapped the handcuff closed on it. He helped Liam to his feet and laced his fingers with the other man's. He led Liam, and they walked across the parking lot, hand in hand.

# CHAPTER NINETEEN

Dawson had been going in and out of sleep, half-dreaming. She had heard the phone ring through the walls, and then heard the cadence of Liam's voice, and incorporated it all into her dreams.

She dreamed that she was driving and that Liam was talking.

She drove through the town, past Renwick Hall, past Destiny's old apartment, past the parking lot. In her dream, these things were all on the same block, one right after the other. She was driving the car, and Liam was in the passenger's seat.

He was talking to someone in the back seat.

Dawson checked her rearview mirror.

Slater was there, grinning his wide, easy grin, showing all his teeth.

She came fully awake with a start, her heart pounding.

She sat up in bed and took several deep breaths, trying to calm herself.

That was when she realized she couldn't hear Liam's voice anymore.

She got out of bed and knocked softly on the adjoining door between their rooms. "Liam?" she called.

He didn't answer, so she knocked again.

When she got nothing, she turned the knob. It wasn't locked, so she slowly eased it open.

The first things she saw was his bed, the covers askew. He wasn't in his bed.

She pushed forward into the room, and took in the closet door, which was wide open. "Liam?"

No answer.

She checked the bathroom. Not there. Well, maybe he'd gone for a walk or something. Maybe he hadn't been able to sleep. She went back into her room and called his cell phone.

"Liam's phone," someone that wasn't Liam answered cheerily.

It took her a moment to place the voice, but then it settled in the pit of her stomach like a stone. "Slater."

"According to Liam's contacts, this is Detective Dawson calling," said Slater. "Is that right? Your voice is so deep over the phone. Do people call you 'sir' all the time? Does that just tick you off?"

"Where's Liam?"

"I googled you," said Slater. "It took a little bit, but I figured I'd be finding a male name. But imagine my delight and surprise when your female name got hits too, from years ago when you were in high school. What an interesting person you are, detective. No wonder Liam has a thing for you."

She licked her lips. "I don't think you've had enough time to take him far away. You must be close."

"You're actually quite the detective," said Slater. "Your record for recovering stolen items is exceptional. I'm impressed with you, too. I might have a thing for you myself. But you may have realized that Liam and I are a package deal."

"I'm going to find you," she said.

"I have no doubt of that," said Slater. "See you soon, then. Bye, now, Haysle." He hung up.

Dawson dialed Liam again.

Straight to voicemail.

She paced for a minute, trying to think, and then she decided she needed to call someone at the local department. The problem was that her contact there was Householder, who was pretty hung up on her own guilt in the case, and Dawson didn't want to bother her. So, she called the main line and introduced herself to man who answered the phone. "The man I came here with has been captured by Phineas Slater, and I need backup," she told him.

"Uh… well, it's the middle of the night here," he said. "There are some guys patrolling the campus, and I could see if I could get permission to pull them in?"

"Fine," she said. "Do that."

"Okay," he said. "I'll call you back. Where do you want me to send them?"

She didn't know the answer to that yet. "I'll tell you when you call me back."

"Okay," he said again. "Talk to you soon." He hung up the phone.

Dawson got dressed and left her hotel room. She stared at the numbers on the elevator as they counted down and willed the answer to come to her. Nothing was coming to her.

She stared at her phone, willing someone from the local department to call her back.

No one did.

She thought about calling someone in Cape Christopher, but what were they supposed to do? They were hours away. She thought about calling Householder, anyway. Householder might be some help.

Had she only dreamed Liam had been on the phone or had that really happened? Who'd called him? Slater?

No, that didn't make sense. If Slater had called him, that would indicate that Liam had gone to him willingly, and he wouldn't have done that. Maybe…

Had there been a new chapter posted on the fanfic?

The elevator door opened and spit her out on the bottom floor of the hotel. She left the elevator and sat down in the lobby to check the fanfiction site. There *was* a new chapter.

She dialed Hernandez. When he answered, she said, "Sorry to wake you, but Liam Emerson is missing."

"Missing? What? I just talked to him," said Hernandez. "I wasn't asleep by the way."

"So, you called him? About the new chapter?"

"Yeah, I said that I would," said Hernandez.

"What did you two talk about?"

"He, um, well, the chapter is really disturbing," said Hernandez. "See, what Joe does is capture Frank and tie him to this chair, and there's this banquet of people there for them to eat, because, see, Joe is a vampire, and Frank can feed off of people to strengthen his magic, and it's also really sexual, and there's a lot of blood, and—"

"This is not helping me," she interrupted. "Is there anything in the chapter that might indicate where Slater would be with Liam?"

"You think Liam was captured?"

"I know it," she said. "I talked to Slater on the phone."

"Shit," said Hernandez in a tiny voice. "The things that Joe does to Frank are—"

"Where?"

"Uh…" Hernandez's voice wasn't strong. "Okay, well we talked about how it was analogous to the dorm where they lived, Renwick Hall?"

"That place is falling down."

"I know, that's what Liam said. And then I said this thing about a place where both of the guys—Joe and Frank—had sex with Cindy, but that didn't have anything analogous—"

"The bunker," she said. "But we can't *find* the bunker." She sighed. "Okay, well, I'm going to go out to Renwick, then. I don't know where else to go."

"Okay," said Hernandez. "Is there anything I can do?"

"I don't think so."

"But I want to help," he said.

Her phone beeped at her.

"Hernandez, I've got another call. I need to go." She hung up and answered. "Dawson."

"Hi, Detective Dawson, we just spoke on the phone. I've got permission to send three other officers to your location. Where should I send them?"

"Renwick Hall," she said, even though she knew it wasn't right.

* * *

Dawson arrived at Renwick before any of the other police officers. She climbed up over the broken-down porch and peered in through the gaping door.

The place was badly damaged by the fire that had raged within. Parts of the upper floors had collapsed, as well as the roof. No one was in there. There was nowhere in there to be.

She backed out of the place and waited, hoping someone would show up.

And then she remembered something.

Householder had reported that Slater had come out from underneath the porch in Renwick Hall when he'd taken Kaveney hostage. Dawson had a flashlight with her, and she shined her light under the porch.

There.

There was a hole there, a hole big enough for a person to crawl inside.

*That* was the way into the bunker. Truthfully, this dorm wasn't that far from the parking lot. She should have seen this before.

She waited for a few minutes for her backup to show up, but they still weren't there, and she felt like she was wasting time. She called the main number for the department again, but it was busy.

She debated.

Going down there on her own with no one else was

stupid.

But it wasn't as if she had to stop trying to call the main number while she went through the underground tunnel. Someone would pick up before she actually made it to the bunker, and as long as someone knew where she was, and was coming for her, it wasn't stupid at all.

She was sure that she could keep Slater talking if she had to. He was the one who said he liked to monologue.

Decided, she climbed under the porch and crawled into the tunnel. She expected to lower herself down, but instead, it descended at a steep incline. It wasn't tall enough for her to stand. She had to crawl.

She did this for about a hundred feet, shining the flashlight ahead of herself to illuminate only more tunnel ahead. The tunnel was dirt on all sides. Every now and again, tree roots descended into it.

She thought about animals that might be down here and then she thought about things that slithered.

Best try to call the department.

She dialed.

Still busy.

Damn it.

She continued a few more feet.

She paused, getting her phone out to try to call again.

Hmm. She didn't seem to have service now. That was odd. Was she too far underground? She crawled back up a few feet, to the spot where she'd called from before.

Still no service.

Damn it.

She should crawl out of the tunnel now. She should go up and wait for backup.

*It's stupid to keep going, Haysle. The last time you faced this guy, he got your gun and your car.*

Yeah, true, but that was before she'd faced the Jane Doe and pulled the trigger without hesitation. That was before she'd found her deep well of calm in the face of panic.

*I can do this,* she thought to herself.

Deliberately, she turned around and began to crawl again.

The tunnel seemed to go on forever. She crawled and crawled, holding the flashlight in her mouth at some points, and then moving it to her hand and bracing it against the dirt floor.

She expected something awful to come out at her—a snake or a large spindly-legged spider or even just a wriggling worm.

There was nothing but dirt.

As she went on, sweat broke out on the back of her neck. Perhaps because of exertion, or because it was warmer underground or because she was nervous.

She began to wonder if this tunnel led anywhere at all.

And then, in the distance, she saw a light.

Her heart stuttered.

She switched off her flashlight and paused to take her gun out and make sure that it was loaded. Then, she tried her phone again. Still no service. She put her phone away and gripped her gun. Now, instead of bracing her flashlight against the dirt floor, she braced her weapon. Because of the awkwardness of crawling with it, she kept the safety on.

She inched forward, toward that light.

It was an orangey sort of glow, and under any other circumstances, it might have seemed comforting. But this light promised anything but comfort.

As she approached, she began to hear voices.

She couldn't make out what they were saying. They were both male, and soon enough, she recognized them as belonging to Slater and Liam.

The orange light was spilling out of a hole in the tunnel up ahead, and the voices were too. Eventually, she was close. She slowed, scooting herself up off her hands and knees as quietly as she could.

She clutched the gun to her chest.

She put her back against the wall of the tunnel and slowly turned, leading with her gun.

But there was no one in the small room of the bunker, only orange light from a kerosene lantern on the floor. The room was full of shelves that strained under the weight of old, dusty cans and jars.

"Oh," said Slater's voice. "That'll be Dawson. Come on through, detective. I knew you'd make it."

She eased her way forward, gun first.

The shelf room opened onto a different room. This was the bunk room that Liam had described. The bunks were folded up against the walls. There was a mattress against one of the walls and a set of woman's clothing was crumpled up on it. It looked dirty and old, as though it had been there a long time.

In the center of the room, a card table had been set up and two chairs. Liam was tied to one of the chairs, his back to the open doorway. Slater was sitting on the other side with a long, sharp kitchen knife grasped in his hand. He pointed it at Dawson.

On the table, there was an array of food in open takeout containers. Mounds of fried chicken, piles of mashed potatoes and gravy, heaps of macaroni and cheese, and towers of cupcakes. There was also a little case open, containing a syringe, a few small bottles of liquid and two glinting needles.

That was right. She remembered this. Slater had access to various injectable drugs which he'd stolen from a hospital where one of his ex-boyfriends worked. Apparently, he had some hidden away that the police hadn't found when they'd confiscated the others for evidence. So, maybe Slater planned to knock them out and leave them alive. Or to knock her out and take Liam.

Well, that wasn't going to happen. She was taking

Slater in. He was going back to jail.

Liam had turned to look at her when she came in. His hands were handcuffed together and he had a chicken leg in one hand, one bite out of it. He was chewing.

Dawson aimed her gun at Slater and pulled the trigger.

And nothing happened, because the safety was on.

Slater sprang across the room and put the tip of the blade he held against the back of Liam's skull.

Liam closed his eyes and dropped the chicken leg. "Now?" he breathed.

"Relax, tiger," said Slater. "It only hurts for a little bit."

"Liar," said Liam.

Slater chuckled. "Give me your gun, detective."

She had taken the safety off now, but she wasn't pulling the trigger, because she didn't know if she could do it before Slater stabbed Liam.

"Just hold it by the barrel and hand it over," said Slater. "You can put the safety back on if it makes you feel better."

"No," she said. She couldn't hand over the gun. The other officers did not know where she was. She was on her own down here. But she also couldn't allow anything to happen to Liam. Even if she didn't have confusing quasi-romantic feelings toward him, it was her job to protect him, and she took that very seriously.

"Don't you want to know what happened to Destiny Worth, detective?" said Slater. "If you don't hand me that gun, you'll never find out. And I'll have to kill Liam here, and that's going to make me really ticked off, because I *like* Liam, a lot. I'll have to take that out on you, and I'll have to make you suffer before I kill you. I don't think you'll like that."

"Just do it, Haysle," said Liam in a low voice. "There's no resisting him. You have to see that."

"Give me the gun, and I'll tell you all about it."

"Do you have to?" said Liam.

"Yes, tiger," said Slater, and he traced the tip of the knife down the back of Liam's neck, caressing the notches of his spine. "I'm afraid so."

Liam sighed, shivering, almost pleasurably.

"Gun," said Slater, holding out his hand.

She shook her head.

Suddenly, Slater lunged.

She pulled the trigger, but the shot didn't hit anything, because she'd been aiming in the spot where Slater no longer was. The bullet pinged against the bottom of one of the bunks and then buried itself in the ceiling above her head.

And while that was happening, Slater was on her, slicing the knife into her forearm with one hand, and prying the gun away from her with the other.

She shrieked in shock and pain and stared at the red line of blood on her arm.

Slater handed her a napkin from the table and gestured to the mattress on the floor. "Have a seat, detective."

She pressed the napkin to her wound.

Slater turned the gun on her.

She hated herself. She was stupid. There was no reason on earth to have come down here on her own, and she must have known it deep down when she'd made the decision to come into the bunker. *I couldn't have told anyone? Not even Hernandez? Not even Householder?*

She was too stupid to survive. She deserved a bullet from her own gun.

But Liam…

Liam didn't deserve this.

Slater returned to the other side of the table, keeping the gun trained on her, but his gaze on Liam.

Liam drew in a breath. "You want me to eat?"

"Yes," hissed Slater.

"What?" said Liam.

"I want you to eat the macaroni," said Slater. "Slow, while I tell Haysle about what you did to Destiny. Very slow. Enjoy it."

Liam reached out for the container and fished a plastic fork off the table. He began to eat the macaroni and cheese.

"Liam strangled Destiny to death," Slater said. He pointed to the mattress where Dawson was sitting. "It happened right there. Right where you're sitting, detective."

Dawson glanced down at the dingy mattress, at the old stains on it. And then her gaze fell on the crumpled pile of clothes.

"That's what she was wearing," said Slater. "You'll take the clothes with you, detective, and have them tested, and you'll find Destiny Worth's DNA."

Dawson swallowed. She didn't know what this game was, or why Slater was telling her this, but she didn't believe it. Liam hadn't killed Destiny. Slater had. On the other hand, if Dawson was taking clothes with her, then Slater intended for her to survive. Interesting. She didn't understand this game at all.

"She wasn't actually wearing any clothes when she died," said Slater. "None of us were."

Liam chewed and swallowed the macaroni.

"How's it taste?" said Slater.

"Good," said Liam.

"You always liked it with pepper," said Slater, whose voice had taken on a loose quality. "Put some pepper on it."

Liam picked up a pepper shaker and began to douse the macaroni and cheese.

"Tell the detective that I'm telling her the truth. That it was you who killed Destiny."

Liam shoved macaroni into his mouth instead.

Slater made a tsk sound, displeased. He turned his attention on Dawson. "You see, it had never been that way for me before. I'd never killed anyone. Liam knows what I did. I always let the girls go. But then… this happened. He choked the life out of her and gave her to me."

Dawson glared at him. "Bullshit."

Slater smiled at her. "Isn't that how it happened, tiger?"

"No," said Liam.

Slater turned his attention back to Liam. "Now, now, tell the detective the truth. Tell her what you did."

"I didn't give her to you," said Liam.

"You killed her for me, didn't you? It *was* for me."

Liam stuck his fork in the macaroni and cheese and sat back in his chair. "I never meant for her to be dead."

Slater groaned. "Really? We're still at this roadblock? You're going to tell me it was an accident?"

"It…" Liam clasped his handcuffed hands together and set them on the table. "It doesn't matter what you make me say, Finn. It's under duress. I'm afraid for my life, and I'm afraid of what you might do to Dawson, so whatever I say means nothing."

Dawson looked back and forth between the two men, neither of whom were paying much attention to her at this moment. She needed to use this. She wasn't handcuffed or tied to a chair. She needed to find a weapon, incapacitate Slater, and get Liam the hell out of here.

Her gaze swept the room, but she only saw the bunks and the table. Maybe one of the chairs might work, but she'd have to get one of the men out of the chairs.

"You told me you wanted me to kill you, tiger," said Slater, sounding wounded. "Are you going to take that back now and fight me?"

"Do you want me to fight you?"

"Maybe," said Slater, his voice dropping in register. "You also said I could do things to you. Maybe we should have… a wrestling match. We can fight to see who gets to be on top."

"Let Dawson go," said Liam. "Why do you have to drag her into it?"

"I can't simply let her go," said Slater in a gentle voice, as if he was explaining something very complicated to a small child. "She'll go and get more cops."

"They're already on their way," said Dawson.

Slater turned to her, studying her expression for several minutes.

"She's lying," said Liam. "Look at me. What do you want me to say again? What do you want me to tell her?"

"Tell her what you did to Destiny," said Slater. "I think I made that pretty clear."

"I strangled her," said Liam. "I choked her until she stopped breathing. She let me do it because she thought we were doing erotic asphyxiation.  It was a thing we did sometimes."

"Don't tell me," said Slater. "Tell her."

Liam turned to Dawson. "I killed Destiny Worth."

Slater sighed. "I don't see why that was so hard."

Liam held her gaze.

*I'm lying about the backup,* she thought at him. *No one's coming. You can distract Slater all you want, you can play along with him, but we're on our own here.*

"You stopped eating." Slater sounded sulky. "You said you'd eat for me."

"Sorry," said Liam, going back to the macaroni and cheese.

"Cupcakes," said Slater. "Eat the chocolate."

Liam pushed the macaroni and cheese away and picked up a chocolate cupcake. He slowly pulled aside the wrapper.

Slater watched, tilting his chin back.

Liam's tongue darted out. He licked the chocolate icing.

Slater made a noise in the back of his throat.

Dawson needed to be doing something. Could she knock Liam out of his chair and then hurl it at Slater? Doubtful. Slater still had the gun. She wouldn't be able to move quickly enough.

Liam sank his teeth into the cupcake.

Slater sucked in a noisy breath.

Maybe Slater's chair. He'd go down. That would give her time to pick up the chair. What did she have to lose by trying?

"Now that the detective knows about Destiny," Slater said, "she'll have to arrest you, tiger."

Liam swallowed a bite of cupcake and licked the crumbs off his fingers. "Oh, so now we get to the plan. What is it you want? You want me to kill her? No way. I'm not going to kill with you, Finn."

"I didn't say that." Slater gestured to the syringes. "That's why I brought these. We can just knock her out. Of course, if you *did* want to kill her, I could help you."

"I don't want her dead," said Liam.

"Fine," said Slater, shrugging. "We'll work up to that, tiger. But you'll come with me now. Because whether you kill her or not, you *have* killed. You started this, in fact. You made me what I am. You killed Destiny, and it was a revelation, and I had to do it again and again and again. Her death changed me. It changed you too, but you keep fighting it."

Liam's face twisted. "Are you going to put me in a cage again?"

"No, there won't be any need for that, I hope," said Slater. "You come with me, and the detective can take Destiny's clothes and get them tested, and then…"

"Then you'll own me," said Liam. He turned to look at

Dawson. "Because she'll know everything."

"I already own you," said Slater in a velvet voice.

Liam took a shaky breath. "Take the cuffs off me."

"Why would I do that?"

"So, that I can kill Detective Dawson, of course."

# CHAPTER TWENTY

Liam didn't like the way Dawson reacted. She didn't seem frightened, and she needed to seem frightened, so he was going to have to convince them both that he was serious.

"Fine," he growled. "I'll do it with the cuffs on, but you can at least untie me from the chair."

Finn looked him over. "I told you before that I can't trust you, tiger."

"You don't need to trust me," said Liam. "Hell, we'll probably have to have that little wrestling match you were talking about, because maybe I'm not in the mood to be owned anymore, Finn. Maybe I want free. Maybe I want on top."

Finn narrowed his eyes.

"It's not about you, it's about her," said Liam. He turned his attention to Dawson. "Told you I'd be bad for you, didn't I, Haysle?"

She regarded him coolly.

"I didn't like killing her, and I'm not going to enjoy killing you," he said. "Finn and I are different that way. I won't let him violate your corpse, if it's any consolation."

Dawson flinched.

Good.

"Untie me, Finn, now," said Liam.

Finn got up from the table, bringing over his knife. He hesitated for a moment, and then he knelt down and cut away the rope that tied Liam's feet to the chair. Then he cut the rope that tied Liam's torso.

"You could shoot her and save us both some trouble," said Liam.

"Is that what you want?" said Finn, pointing the gun at Dawson.

Except Dawson wasn't there anymore.

Liam turned to see that she'd run to snatch up Finn's chair. She brought it down on Finn's back with a crash.

The chair splintered, and Finn faltered for a moment before turning on Dawson with a roar.

Liam took that opportunity to tackle Finn, and they went backwards into the table, food flying everywhere. He went for the gun.

He and Finn struggled over it.

Then he felt the point of the knife under his ribs.

Finn's voice was regretful. "How many times am I going to let you break my heart, tiger? I keep thinking this time, I'm going to get you back, and you always disappoint me."

Liam breathed.

Finn pushed the tip of the knife into Liam's skin.

Liam cried out.

Finn's mouth was on his as the knife went deeper.

Dawson kicked Finn in the side of the face.

Finn brought up the gun and shot her.

She crumpled to the ground, motionless.

Liam made a strangled noise, clutching his wound. He didn't think it was that deep. He didn't think any of his organs had been pierced, but he was bleeding, and it hurt. He crawled toward Dawson.

Finn stopped him. He was on his feet now, and he put his boot into Liam's back, crunching him into the cold, concrete floor.

Liam grunted.

"You're going to take the needle now," said Finn.

"I need to check on Dawson," he said. "I need to see if

she's..."

Finn shifted all of his weight onto the foot on Liam's back.

Liam groaned in pain.

"You're going to take the needle, tiger," Finn said softly. He stepped off Liam's back and was back in seconds with a syringe. "Don't fight," he said. "We'll do that next time." He ran a hand through Liam's hair affectionately.

Liam tried to struggle, but his wound pulsed and bled and Finn punched the needle into his vein and...

Dark.

# CHAPTER TWENTY-ONE

First, they got drunk that night, and then they went to the bunker.

When Destiny started tugging at Liam's clothes, he tried to tell her that it was pointless because he'd had way too many shots, and there was no way he could even possibly achieve an erection. Besides which, Finn was there, and Finn would be weirded out by it all.

Except Finn was drunk too, and he wasn't weird. He just laughed, and put his hand down the front of Liam's pants, and Liam was too drunk to protest.

They undressed him, both of them. Destiny peeled off his jeans and Finn unbuttoned his shirt.

And he was drunk.

So, so drunk.

Things were spinning, and he was going in and out of consciousness, and everything seemed to be swirling past him. It was almost as if things were happening to him, and he was outside it all, just watching it.

He watched himself kissing Destiny and kissing Finn, and he watched himself putting his hands under Destiny's shirt, and then—

He time-traveled to the future.

In the future, Destiny was not wearing clothes, and Finn was only in his boxers, and Finn was kissing Liam, and running his hands over Liam's chest, and Destiny's hands were on Liam's crotch, and the future was good.

Liam liked the future.

Everything whirled and swirled again, and he was lost to pleasure and drunkenness and confusion.

There was another gap, another stretch of time in which he time-traveled.

He came to himself in *pain*.

Sharp, agonizing hot pain that woke him up, sobering him immediately.

He was inside Destiny, and she had her legs wrapped around his hips.

Finn's voice was at Liam's ear, a scratchy, drunken whisper. "Relax, tiger. It only hurts for a little bit."

Liam couldn't breathe. The pain was scalding. It was splitting him in two. It was the worst thing he'd ever felt in his entire life. "Don't," he managed.

Finn's hand soothed its way down Liam's spine. "You'll get used to it."

"You're hard, Liam," said Destiny, who was wriggling her hips against him. "I've never felt you so big or hard."

And that was true, as far as that went, although he couldn't understand why, because he couldn't feel any part of his body except... except *Finn's* body, which was burning him from the inside out, which was huge and painful and insistent.

"Stop." Liam's voice broke. "Please. Finn? Stop."

Destiny kissed him.

"You said you wanted it," Finn was murmuring.

"I don't remember saying that," Liam protested. He tried to move, but moving was agony, and so he just stayed still, and he was trapped in this awful place, this bad, dark, pain place.

Destiny ran her fingers over Liam's chest. "Choke me."

"Yeah," agreed Finn's dark voice at his ear. "Put your hands on her."

Liam bowed his head, resting his forehead on Destiny's shoulder. He wanted to cry. He didn't understand how this had happened. He didn't understand how the pleasant drunken swirling world had turned into this, and most of all, he didn't know how to make it stop. "I don't like this," he said, but his voice was muffled against Destiny's skin, and Finn was starting to move against—*inside*—him, and the hell of it was that it *didn't* hurt as much anymore, that maybe he *was* getting used to it.

Even still, it wasn't good, even if something about it was starting to become physically pleasurable, even if Destiny's hips were thrusting against him, even if he was cresting toward something.

Suddenly, he was angry.

He wrapped his hands around Destiny's neck.

"*Yes.*" She grinned at him. "Is it good, Liam? Do you like it when we fuck you?"

"Shut up," he said, and he squeezed.

He squeezed hard, harder than he'd ever squeezed, and his climax came on him like a bullet in a gun. It exploded out of his body, and he was still squeezing, still crushing her neck, and then—

He blacked out again, but when he woke up, he was lying next to Destiny on the mattress, but Finn was inside her.

Liam watched that, watched that go on and on and thought about how Destiny wasn't moving or talking or responding or… or breathing?

"Stop it, Finn," he said. "Stop it."

Finn didn't stop.

Liam grabbed him by the shoulders. "What the fuck is going on?" he shouted.

Finn kissed him.

Liam shoved him away. He stumbled out to find his clothes and he climbed out of the bunker. He remembered being out in the field, looking up at the stars, wondering what time it was.

And then he blacked out again and he woke up in Destiny's apartment and it was morning.

He told himself it must have all been some kind of awful dream, and that Destiny would be down in the kitchen, making coffee and wearing one of his t-shirts and that Finn would be in the guest room, and that nothing like that could possibly have ever happened.

But Destiny never came back to the apartment, and eventually Liam went back to his dorm room.

They still lived in Renwick, but they had a bigger room now, one on the first floor that was intended for four people. Since they were seniors, they'd snagged it as a double.

Finn was lounging on his bed with laptop. "Morning, tiger," he said when Liam came in. He didn't even look up.

Liam just gaped at him.

Finn stared at the screen. "I guess it's really afternoon, isn't it? Not morning."

"What happened last night?" Liam said to him.

Finn glanced up over the top of the laptop. "Don't you remember?"

"I don't know what I remember," said Liam.

"Me either," said Finn, shrugging.

"Where's Destiny?" said Liam.

Finn smirked at him. "Really, tiger?"

Liam swallowed.

Finn went back to his laptop.

Liam advanced on him and slammed it closed. "Don't be like that."

Finn cocked his head to one side. "You ran off and left me to deal with it."

Liam started to shake. "Deal with what?"

"You want me to say it out loud?" said Finn. "Don't worry, tiger. I took care of it."

Liam took a step back.

"The words you might be looking for are, 'thank you.'" Finn smiled, and the smile was wrong somehow.

Liam took another step back. "Don't... don't ever touch me again."

He went and threw a bunch of clothes into one of his duffel bags and left the room. He didn't go back there, not alone, for the rest of the year.

# CHAPTER TWENTY-TWO

Dawson woke up with a dry mouth, feeling woozy from loss of blood. As far as the gunshot went, it wasn't bad. It had gone through and through the fleshy part of her arm. It was the kind of shot that—in the movies— would only make the hero stumble for a few seconds before she righted herself, switched her gun to her other hand, and pumped the bad guy full of lead.

But people who wrote movie scripts had never felt an actual gun shot.

It *hurt*.

She'd never been shot before, and maybe it was the shock of it more than anything that had downed her. By the time she was over it enough to even think about gathering herself together and trying to fight, Slater was sticking her vein with a needle, and she had immediately lost consciousness.

Now, Slater was gone.

Liam was still there. His clothes were spattered in remnants of the food, which was spilled all over the inside of the bunker. He was bleeding. His shirt was full of blood. He was moving and conscious, though, making his way painfully towards her.

She sat up, looking him over.

Liam drew in a breath. "You're alive."

"Yeah." She looked him over. "So are you."

He looked down at the place where his hand was pressed to his bloody shirt. "Hurts like hell."

"We have to get out of here," she said. "I guess that means we have to crawl through that damned tunnel."

"Do you have a phone?" he said.

"No service," she said. But then she yanked it out anyway and turned it on.

"He took mine," grunted Liam.

"No, I know, because I called you."

"Oh, yeah," said Liam. "I almost forgot about that."

She looked at the screen. She had a bar. Maybe… She dialed the number for the local police. Nothing happened.

She switched the phone to her other hand and raised it high above her head.

Nothing.

She forced herself to her feet, getting the phone even higher…

And she heard the sound of the phone dialing.

She let out a little laugh and put the phone to her ear. When the man she'd spoken to before answered, she said, "This is Detective Dawson, and I—

"Dawson, we've been looking everywhere for you."

"I'm in a bunker that's accessed from a tunnel that starts under the porch at Renwick Hall," she said. "I've been shot, and Liam Emerson has been stabbed. We need medical attention."

"Slater?"

"He's gone," she said. "I should have waited for backup. I'm an idiot."

No response.

She looked at the phone. She'd lost service again. She sank painfully back down to the floor. "I guess we should start crawling toward them. It's not as if they're going to be able to put you on a stretcher and carry you through that tunnel."

Liam gestured at the phone. "Did he hang up on you?"

"Service cut out," she said.

"Oh," he said. He gritted his teeth in pain. "Listen, those things Finn made me say—"

"I understood when you said that you were only doing what he wanted," she said.

"I never hurt Destiny," he said. "I would never have done that."

She eyed him, and she didn't say anything.

"Do you believe me?"

"If it was an accident, Liam—"

"*He* did it," said Liam. "I mean, I guess. I don't know. When I left this bunker, she was alive."

She nodded slowly. "Let's just get out of here, okay?"

"I need to know you don't believe him."

"If there was no truth to it, then why did he think that it would make you go with him?" she said.

"I don't know," said Liam. "He's insane."

She nodded again. "He is. Yes, he's clearly detached from reality."

"He tried to frame me before," said Liam. "This is what he wants. He wants to take everything away from me. He wants to make people doubt me. He wants him and me to be the same, and we're not the same, so he thinks he can make me like him. But I swear to you, I never hurt Destiny. *Never.*"

She reached out and put a reassuring hand on his shoulder. "Of course you didn't. Of course I believe you, Liam."